Catrina had been asleep for five hours. Rick would probably be ready to kill her.

The television was on in the living room. Catrina shaded her eyes and saw the top of a head barely visible above the back of the sofa.

With her heart pounding, she quietly walked around the sofa and nearly melted at what she saw. There was Rick Blaine, with orange stains on his shirt and spaghetti stuck to his hair, cradling the squeaky-clean, pajama-clad toddler in his arms. Both were sound asleep.

For a moment, Catrina just stood there, unable to trust her own eyes. Never in her life had she seen anything that touched her so deeply. This was the real Rick Blaine, she realized. Not the glib genius, not the brilliant bachelor. In one vulnerable, unguarded moment, she had glimpsed the soul of a man who had the power to change her life forever.

Dear Reader,

This holiday season, as our anniversary year draws to a close, we have much to celebrate. The talented authors who have published—and continue to publish—unforgettable love stories. You, the readers, who have made our twenty-year milestone possible. And this month's very special offerings.

First stop: BACHELOR GULCH, Sandra Steffen's popular ongoing miniseries. They'd shared an amazing night together; now a beguiling stranger was back in his life carrying *Sky's Pride and Joy*. She'd dreamed *Hunter's Vow* would be the marrying kind...until he learned about their child he'd never known existed—don't miss this keeper by Susan Meier! Carolyn Zane's BRUBAKER BRIDES are back! *Montana's Feisty Cowgirl* thought she could pass as just another *male* ranch hand, but Montana wouldn't rest till he knew her secrets...and made this 100% woman completely his!

Donna Clayton's SINGLE DOCTOR DADS return...STAT. *Rachel and the M.D.* were office assistant and employer...so why was she imagining herself this widower's bride and his triplets' mother? Diana Whitney brings her adorable STORK EXPRESS series from Special Edition into Romance with the delightful story of what happens when *Mixing Business...with Baby*. And debut author Belinda Barnes tells the charming tale of a jilted groom who finds himself all dressed up...to deliver a pregnant beauty's baby—don't miss *His Special Delivery!*

Thank you for celebrating our 20th anniversary. In 2001 we'll have even more excitement—the return of ROYALLY WED and Marie Ferrarella's 100th book, to name a couple!

Happy reading!

Mary-Theresa Hussey
Senior Editor

Please address questions and book requests to:
Silhouette Reader Service
U.S.: 3010 Walden Ave., P.O. Box 1325, Buffalo, NY 14269
Canadian: P.O. Box 609, Fort Erie, Ont. L2A 5X3

Mixing Business...with Baby

DIANA WHITNEY

Published by Silhouette Books

America's Publisher of Contemporary Romance

If you purchased this book without a cover you should be aware that this book is stolen property. It was reported as "unsold and destroyed" to the publisher, and neither the author nor the publisher has received any payment for this "stripped book."

To Cinderella dreams,
and those who dare believe in them.

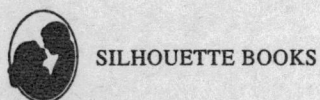 SILHOUETTE BOOKS

ISBN 0-373-19490-0

MIXING BUSINESS...WITH BABY

Copyright © 2000 by Diana Hinz

All rights reserved. Except for use in any review, the reproduction or utilization of this work in whole or in part in any form by any electronic, mechanical or other means, now known or hereafter invented, including xerography, photocopying and recording, or in any information storage or retrieval system, is forbidden without the written permission of the editorial office, Silhouette Books, 300 East 42nd Street, New York, NY 10017 U.S.A.

All characters in this book have no existence outside the imagination of the author and have no relation whatsoever to anyone bearing the same name or names. They are not even distantly inspired by any individual known or unknown to the author, and all incidents are pure invention.

This edition published by arrangement with Harlequin Books S.A.

® and TM are trademarks of Harlequin Books S.A., used under license. Trademarks indicated with ® are registered in the United States Patent and Trademark Office, the Canadian Trade Marks Office and in other countries.

Visit Silhouette at www.eHarlequin.com

Printed in U.S.A.

Books by Diana Whitney

Silhouette Romance

O'Brian's Daughter #673
A Liberated Man #703
Scout's Honor #745
The Last Bachelor #874
One Man's Vow #940
One Man's Promise #1307
††A Dad of His Own #1392
‡Mixing Business...
　with Baby #1490

Silhouette Intimate Moments

Still Married #491
Midnight Stranger #530
Scarlet Whispers #603

Silhouette Shadows

The Raven Master #31

*The Blackthorn Brotherhood
†Parenthood
‡Stork Express
††For the Children

Silhouette Special Edition

Cast a Tall Shadow #508
Yesterday's Child #559
One Lost Winter #644
Child of the Storm #702
The Secret #874
*The Adventurer #934
*The Avenger #984
*The Reformer #1019
†Daddy of the House #1052
†Barefoot Bride #1073
†A Hero's Child #1090
‡Baby on His Doorstep #1165
‡Baby in His Cradle #1176
Who's That Baby? #1205
††I Now Pronounce You Mom
　& Dad #1261
††The Fatherhood Factor #1276
‡Baby of Convenience #1361

Silhouette Books

36 Hours
Ooh Baby, Baby

DIANA WHITNEY

A three-time Romance Writers of America RITA Award finalist, *Romantic Times Magazine* Reviewers' Choice nominee and finalist for Colorado Romance Writers' Award of Excellence, Diana Whitney has published more than two dozen romance and suspense novels since her first Silhouette title in 1989. A popular speaker, Diana has conducted writing workshops, and has published several articles on the craft of fiction-writing for various trade magazines and newsletters. She is a member of the Authors Guild, Novelists, Inc., Published Authors Network and Romance Writers of America. She and her husband live in rural Northern California with a beloved menagerie of furred creatures, domestic and wild. She loves to hear from readers. You can write to her c/o Silhouette Books, 300 East 42nd Street, 6th Floor, New York, NY 10017.

IT'S OUR 20th ANNIVERSARY!

December 2000 marks the end of our anniversary year. We hope you've enjoyed the many special titles already offered, and we invite you to sample those wonderful titles on sale this month! 2001 promises to be every bit as exciting, so keep coming back to Silhouette Books, where love comes alive....

Desire

#1333 Irresistible You
Barbara Boswell

#1334 Slow Fever
Cait London

#1335 A Season for Love
BJ James

#1336 Groom of Fortune
Peggy Moreland

#1337 Monahan's Gamble
Elizabeth Bevarly

#1338 Expecting the Boss's Baby
Leanne Banks

Romance

#1486 Sky's Pride and Joy
Sandra Steffen

#1487 Hunter's Vow
Susan Meier

#1488 Montana's Feisty Cowgirl
Carolyn Zane

#1489 Rachel and the M.D.
Donna Clayton

#1490 Mixing Business...with Baby
Diana Whitney

#1491 His Special Delivery
Belinda Barnes

Special Edition

#1363 The Delacourt Scandal
Sherryl Woods

#1364 The McCaffertys: Thorne
Lisa Jackson

#1365 The Cowboy's Gift-Wrapped Bride
Victoria Pade

#1366 Lara's Lover
Penny Richards

#1367 Mother in a Moment
Allison Leigh

#1368 Expectant Bride-To-Be
Nikki Benjamin

Intimate Moments

#1045 Special Report
Merline Lovelace/Maggie Price/Debra Cowan

#1046 Strangers When We Married
Carla Cassidy

#1047 A Very...Pregnant New Year's
Doreen Roberts

#1048 Mad Dog and Annie
Virginia Kantra

#1049 Mirror, Mirror
Linda Randall Wisdom

#1050 Everything But a Husband
Karen Templeton

Chapter One

"I got the job!" Rushing into the tiny, downtown book nook, a breathless Catrina Mitchell Jordan danced the gray-haired proprietor around shelves stacked with leather-bound tomes. "I got the job, I got the job, I got the *job!*"

Her final exuberant trill was completed by the blending of a rumbaesque hip check and the hip-wriggling victory dance of a football player after a game-winning touchdown.

"Of course you got the job." Gracie Applegate chuckled, smoothing a ruffled strand of silver hair back into her gleaming chignon. "There was never a doubt in my mind."

"Well, there was plenty of doubt in my mind. If not for that tip you gave me, I'd still be scouring the want ads and wondering how to pay next month's rent." Suddenly limp with relief, Catrina sagged against the checkout counter fighting foolish tears.

She'd been out of work for weeks, and her meager savings account was nearly drained. "I don't know who you called, or how you managed to work this miracle, but I'm forever in your debt. Thank you so much."

Gracie flicked her wrist as if shooing a pesky fly. "Pish and silliness, child. It's Blaine Architectural that should be thanking me for sending over the best accounts receivable clerk they'll ever lay eyes on. I'm sure my dear friend Martha in the personnel department would agree."

"Is there anyone in Los Angeles that you don't personally know?"

"Oh, I imagine a few folks have slipped past, but one of the perks of owning the finest antique and rare book establishment in the county is the pleasure of meeting lots of lovely, intelligent people. Speaking of which..." Angling a sly glance, she feigned interest in refilling a crystal bowl with fragrant potpourri. "Did you have an opportunity to meet the head honcho himself?"

"Mr. Blaine?" Catrina shook her head, still a bit nervous about meeting the fellow that every employee to whom she'd been introduced had described in the most glowing terms. "Apparently a group of managers had negotiated a lucrative contract to renovate a downtown office complex so he took them all to lunch as a reward."

"How nice. Why are your eyebrows all scrunched up, dear?"

"He took them to lunch in San Francisco, Gracie. Just piled them into a rented plane and flew it himself." Catrina shuddered. "Rich people make me nervous. My sister Laura made the mistake of marrying a rich man. He nearly destroyed her."

Of course, another rich man had galloped to the rescue, just like Prince Charming on the proverbial snow-white steed, although Catrina considered that to be sheer luck.

Gracie tsk-tsked, skimming a disapproving frown in Catrina's direction. "Now, now, dear, you can't judge all well-to-do folks by the actions of a few. Besides, if Rick Blaine were as rich as the rumors imply, he wouldn't have had to rent a plane would he?"

Catrina couldn't help but smile. "No, I suppose not."

A wreath of laugh lines bracketed the older woman's thin mouth, and her blue eyes twinkled with peculiar slyness, as if she knew something that nobody else knew.

And she probably did. Gracie Applegate was a dichotomy, equal parts of grandmotherly wisdom and elfin mischief blended with a pinch of mystery and a dash of clairvoyance. Catrina adored her.

So did Heather.

A cranky gurgle caught Catrina's attention. She moved through the open doorway into the bookstore office to retrieve her sleepy toddler from a playpen that had been set up behind Gracie's desk. "There, there, sweetums, did you have a nice nap?"

The baby's hair was moist and tangled. A reddened pressure mark stained her right cheek. She fussed, stretched, patted Catrina's face. "Gamma Gracie gave me apple."

"Did she now?" Catrina widened her eyes, affectionately exaggerating interest in the mundane information. "That was very nice of Gamma Gracie wasn't it?"

As Heather bobbed her little head in agreement, Catrina angled a questioning glance at the older woman in the doorway.

"Humor an old woman's small pleasures," Gracie replied, displaying her gift for reading Catrina's thoughts. "Since my son has decreed himself a confirmed bachelor for life, the only way I'll ever hear a child call me 'grandma' is if I bribe one to do it. I hope you don't mind."

"Of course I don't mind. Every child needs a doting grandmother. My own mom passed away several years ago, and Heather's paternal grandparents live 3,000 miles away."

"Ah. That's too bad."

"It's for the best. They are nice people, I suppose, but they were never into the grandparent scene. I got the impression that they were relieved enough to have survived raising one child, and weren't anxious to get involved with another one." She shifted the child against her shoulder, nuzzling her soft skin and inhaling the sweet baby fragrance. "Given the pathetic result of their initial foray into parenthood, I can't say as I blame them."

Gracie smiled, but her eyes were sad. "The young man must have had some redeeming characteristics, or an intelligent woman such as yourself wouldn't have married him in the first place."

A warning chill slipped down Catrina's spine. The divorce had been messy, bitter, and the sour taste of failure hung heavily on her tongue. "Dan had always been a sullen, unhappy man. I thought I could change that. I couldn't."

Squeezing her eyes shut, she hugged Heather so tightly that the child squirmed in her arms. She loosened her grip, murmuring soft reassurances as the baby popped a wet thumb back into her mouth. A pang of regret and uncertainty stung Catrina, as it always did when she fretted about how the choices she'd made would affect Heather's future, just as her own mother's choices had affected Catrina's past.

Catrina had grown up without a father. He'd deserted the family when she'd been an infant. That loss had always haunted her. Now it would haunt her beloved daughter too, since Dan hadn't even requested visitation privileges. He'd never really wanted a child.

As it turned out, he'd never wanted a wife, either. He'd wanted a housekeeper, a scapegoat, and a convenient bed partner. Soft footsteps scuffled closer, and she knew Gracie was beside her before she felt the woman's gentle touch on her shoulder. "Sometimes we have to endure the bad times in order to recognize the good ones."

Catrina sniffed, juggled the child in the crook of her arm to free a hand and wipe a stray tear from her own cheek. "I know. But when I think of my daughter growing up with the knowledge that her own father doesn't care about her, it breaks my heart."

Gracie opened her mouth, closed it, and took another moment to consider her words. When she finally spoke, her voice carried a peculiar quiver. "Maybe it just takes some men a while to figure out what's truly important in life. You'll find the right one someday. Just give it time, dear."

"I don't want a man. They cause nothing but heartache and misery, and sooner or later they always walk away. So what's the point?"

"Why, love is the point!"

"Love is a myth."

Gracie made a clucking sound with her tongue. "So young to be so jaded."

"I don't believe in fairy tales, if that's what you mean."

"Of course you don't." Gracie's merry blue eyes twinkled. "That's why you've spent countless hours in my humble establishment poring over great love stories of the ages."

Feeling her skin heat, Catrina shifted her daughter in her arms and shouldered the diaper bag. "Thank you so much for watching Heather. Thank you for everything. Your friendship means so much to me."

Gracie merely responded with a warm smile and a reassuring squeeze on Catrina's shoulder. But as Catrina wound her way through the delicious shelves filled with fanciful tales of love and triumph, a memory echoed inside her head.

You can't count on anyone but yourself, Cattiegirl. The world will break your heart if you let it.

"You were right, Mama," she murmured. "You were so right."

"Please don't toy with me. I'll do anything you want. Anything." Kneeling before that which had imminent power, Catrina leaned in close, whispering softly as her fingertip traced a sensual path downward. "Whatever you want, whatever you need, your wildest fantasy fulfilled. Just grant me this one, teensy favor, and you can name your price." She pressed her cheek against the cool, plastic skin. "Six measley copies, collated and comb-bound before the 3:00 meeting. Your operating manual says you can do this. Please, I'm begging you. I'll polish your glass. I'll vacuum your innards. I'll stack your paper properly and double-check your controls every hour for the rest of my life." She hesitantly pressed the Start button.

The machine whirred, hiccuped, fell silent.

Catrina exhaled all at once. "Or I can smear axle grease on your window, glue your gears together, and let my fingers do the walking through the office equipment pages of the telephone book. The choice is yours, fella. If you cooperate, you live. If not, there's a screwdriver in my desk, and I know how to use it."

A male voice from behind startled the daylights out of her. "I don't know about the machine, but I'm certainly convinced."

Catrina lurched to her feet so abruptly that she caught a heel in the hem of her swingy flowered skirt. With the sick sound of ripped fabric ringing in her ears, she spun to face a tousle-haired man wearing a pair of pleated khaki slacks, a casual golf shirt and a bemused smile.

He stepped back, raised his hands over his head. "Don't hurt me." A smile of uncommon brilliance brightened sky-blue eyes sprinkled with curiosity and sparkling with humor. "Look, I'm unarmed."

Under normal circumstances Catrina would have

appreciated the amusement factor of her bizarre situation. The circumstances, however, were far from normal.

She was tense, feeling both pressured by the expectations of a new job she hadn't yet conquered and embarrassed by having been caught threatening a recalcitrant office machine. "If you don't wish to be implicated in a crime, I suggest you leave the vicinity at once."

The man hiked a brow. "Is there no other way? You don't seem the type to contemplate violence against a helpless collating device."

"Helpless? Ha." Her cheeks burned until she suspected she must be glowing like a neon tomato. "That's what it wants you to believe. It suckers you with its simplistic controls, its benign operating manual, then waits until your entire career is on the line before going in for the kill."

"Is your entire career on the line?"

"If I don't get these reports to the budget committee in the next fifteen minutes it very well may be."

"Hmm, sounds serious." Pursing his lips, he regarded the lumpy device as if actually giving credence to her concern. "Perhaps I can be of assistance. I have some experience with machinery."

"You do?"

"I repaired a lawn mower once."

"How impressive." A covert perusal of his casual attire suggested that he was either an outside vendor or one of the draftsman from the engineering department. "Do you work here?"

The question clearly startled him. "As a matter of fact I do. Why?"

Too exasperated to do more than take vague note of the surprised glint in his eye, she shoved a tangle of hair from her face and glanced at a nearby wall clock. "Because I doubt management would appreciate me giving a non-employee access to company equipment. If you end up destroying the danged thing, I'd personally shake your hand, but the company would either take the replacement cost out of my paycheck or out of my hide. Neither alternative is particularly appealing."

He cocked his head in a manner that was oddly self-effacing and arrogant at the same time. "Then I'll have to be exceptionally gentle, won't I?"

Catrina smiled in spite of her tension. There was a certain charisma about this man that wormed through a person's defenses, a mellow charm that sneaked up slowly, insidiously. Before she could stop herself, she heard herself say, "Blow in its ear, and maybe it will follow you home."

His pupils dilated, darkening into a pool of sensual interest that instantly put her on guard. "Is that all it takes?"

Embarrassed and angry at herself for having fallen into a trap of her own making, she yanked her gaze away and glared at the hapless machine. "If you can make this thing work, I'd appreciate it. Otherwise you'll have to excuse me. There isn't much time for me to make other arrangements."

He recognized her request to depersonalize the conversation and respected it. "I'll see what I can do."

Stepping forward, he opened the access door and peered inside the machine. He hummed, grunted, reached into a cabinet nested in the corner of the alcove and pulled out a stack of tooth-edged plastic templates.

It took a moment for the significance of what he was doing to sink in. When it did, she was mortified. "Please don't tell me that the binder cache was empty."

"All right, I won't tell you." He tapped the stack of plastic edging to square it, then slipped it into the binder cache. "I will simply suggest that when programming a set of instructions, it's helpful if the machine contains all the items necessary to fulfill your request."

With that he pressed the start button, and the machine whirred to life. A minute later, the first neatly-bound report spat out into the holding rack.

Catrina wished the ground would open up and swallow her whole. "Thank you."

"You're welcome."

She didn't have to look at him to know he was smiling. A fresh scent wafted past as he leaned to inspect the results of his handiwork, a masculine blending of soap and cedar that was well suited to his casual, outdoorsy appearance.

Clearing her throat, she angled a glance, realized to her shock that he'd retrieved one of the budget reports from the holding rack and was idly flipping through it.

She immediately plucked it out of his hands. "Are you a member of the budget committee?"

He stared at her as if she'd suddenly sprouted antlers. "Not exactly."

"Then I can't allow you to see this. It's a confidential document."

"I don't think the committee would mind if I took a quick look at the preliminary projections."

"I'm sorry, but company policy forbids the review of budget documents by anyone other than accounting personnel or the budget committee."

"It does?"

"Yes."

"Hmm. I'll have to give the policy manual another look-see."

"That might be prudent." She stacked all of the reports, scooped them into her arms, giddy with relief. Her task was complete, and with five minutes to spare. Life was good. "I suppose I should get these to the conference room."

"Yes, I suppose you should."

She hesitated. She didn't know why. "Thank you again for your help."

There was something incredibly appealing about the way his eyes crinkled at the corners when he smiled. "You're welcome again."

After another moment, she sucked a breath, managed a smile and stepped from the copy-room alcove, nearly colliding with a gray-suited man carrying a thick document tucked under his arm. She stiffened instinctively, snapped to attention as she recognized the company finance director, her boss's boss.

The fellow dodged, spun, touched her shoulder to steady himself. He didn't favor her with a second glance. Instead, his gaze darted around the bustling accounting department with preoccupied verve. "Have you seen Rick?"

"Rick who?"

He blinked, then laughed as if she'd cracked a joke. "That's a good one—" He glanced past her shoulder, toward the copy alcove from which she'd just emerged. "Ah, there you are. Look, the city lawyers are in your office, and I need a signature on these contracts posthaste."

A chill slipped down her spine as the man who'd just witnessed her embarrassing ineptitude with the office machine accepted the proffered documents, flipping through them with practiced skill. "Has the legal department reviewed these?"

The finance director nodded. "Yes, all we need is your approval, and the deal is done."

"Let me give them a quick read first. I'll have Marge hand-carry them to your office when I'm through."

Catrina steadied herself on a metal file cabinet. During the past week of her employment, she'd met dozens of company employees, including most department directors and top managers. She'd met only one person named Marge. She was the personal assistant to the head honcho, one of the few people to whom she had yet to be introduced...the elusive Rick Blaine.

Rick glanced up from the contract long enough to see the color drain from the young woman's face. He'd realized moments earlier that she hadn't known who he was. That hadn't bothered him, actually.

Having just returned from a boring round of golf

with the dull-as-dirt CEO of a national conglomerate in need of a new headquarters complex, Rick realized he looked more like a mail-room employee than the founder of a multimillion dollar architectural firm. He'd always made a point of personally knowing each and every employee of his company. He wondered how this breathtaking young woman had escaped his notice.

The embarrassment in her eyes was quickly replaced by a snap of anger, barely visible before she spun on her heel and marched toward the conference room. A thick gather of toffee-colored hair spilled to her shoulders, bouncing with each hurried step, and the torn hem of her skirt dangled as a reminder of the earlier accident. For some odd reason, the minor disarray of her clothing made him feel strangely protective.

Beside him, the finance manager continued to drone on about the particulars of a contract he'd be reading himself in a few minutes. He interrupted with no particular grace. "Who is that woman?"

"Which woman?" Frank Glasgow blinked, followed his gaze. "Oh, that's our new accounting clerk. Jordan, I believe...Catherine, Caitlin...something like that."

"Find out."

"Find what out?"

Even after the clearly aggravated Ms. Jordan had disappeared into the conference room with her hard-earned stack of budget reports, Rick kept his gaze glued on the vacant doorway, awaiting her return. "Her name. I want to know her name."

"Why?"

"Because it's rude to refer to one's employees as 'hey, you.'"

"Oh." Frank shot a quizzical look, cleared his throat. "Now about the completion clause and noncompliance penalties, I think we should attempt to negotiate a more favorable—"

"Yes, yes, you're quite right," Rick mumbled as the gorgeous Ms. Jordan reappeared in the doorway.

She hesitated, noting his presence with an annoyed sideways glance before hurrying across the spacious open area to a neat desk in front of the management cubicles. She seated herself stiffly, deliberately turned her back on him, a subtle signal that she'd noted his visual interest and rejected it.

"Rick, have you got a moment?"

A vaguely familiar feminine voice caught his attention. He glanced around as a portly, middle-aged woman rushed toward him. "Good afternoon, Sandra. I hear your son's football team won the league championships. Congratulations."

"Thank you. He's up for a sports scholarship at U.C.L.A."

"Really? That's quite a coup. You must be very proud."

"Oh, I am."

"You've done something different with your hair."

"Why, yes." She patted her chic, scissored coiffeur, gave him a grateful smile. "Even my husband didn't notice. Do you like it?"

He flashed her a smile that usually made women flush and giggle. "Extremely attractive. Brings out the resonance of your eyes and draws attention to your lovely smile."

"Flatterer."

"If the truth is flattering, so be it."

Sandra flushed and giggled, then caught herself, clearing her throat and drawing her ample shoulders back with a modicum of dignity. "When you finally get married, you'll break a million hearts, you devil, you."

"Why, I can't possibly get married when the most perfect woman on Earth is already taken." Lifting her hand, he brushed a light kiss across her knuckles, then offered a conspiratorial wink that raised a crimson stain across her cheeks. "I hope your husband realizes what a lucky man he is."

"I'll tell him you said so."

"You do that."

Still blushing madly, Sandra sighed, floated a few steps away, then jerked to a stop. "I almost forgot. The drafting department elected me to express our appreciation for the merit bonus this week. It was very generous of you."

"I'm the one who is appreciative. Please convey my gratitude to your colleagues for a job well done. Because of their efforts, the company was able to secure a lucrative renovation contract that benefits us all."

Sandra was pink with pleasure. "I'll pass that along."

"Please do." Rick gave the woman his undivided attention until she broke visual contact by turning away. Then his gaze immediately returned to the fascinating Ms. Jordan just in time to see her roll her eyes and swivel her chair around until her back was to him again. That she'd been unimpressed by his employee interaction skills couldn't have been more clear if she'd held up a scorecard.

Rick's smile flattened. He wasn't exactly insulted, but he was most certainly confused. People just naturally liked him. They always had, perhaps because he naturally liked them as well.

"It seems as if I've inadvertently gotten off on the wrong foot with our newest employee," he murmured to no one in particular.

"Hmm?" Beside him, Frank followed his gaze and scowled. "She's probably just preoccupied with learning the position. The finance department is one of the most complex and important in the company."

Frank's reminder of his own importance didn't escape Rick's notice. "We couldn't get along without you."

Frank's tailored lapels seemed to puff a bit. He was a short man, thin and balding, with a mustache so neat it appeared to have been trimmed with a template. He was also a man prone to agitation when his ego wasn't routinely stroked, but he was exceptionally good at his job and treated his subordinates with respect. Frank was an excellent manager. Rick appreciated him immensely and would have spent more time stroking that fragile ego if he hadn't been so overwhelmingly intrigued by his own peculiar turmoil.

"We could spend some time discussing those contracts if you'd like," Frank said. "I'm free until 4:30...."

The remainder of Frank's comment dissipated as Rick made a beeline for Ms. Jordan's desk.

The subtle stiffening of her shoulder blades was the only indication that she was aware of Rick's presence. "It occurs to me that we were interrupted before we could complete the introductory process," he said jovially. "I'm Rick Blaine."

"So I gathered." She stared at the computer monitor as if mesmerized by it. Her fingers clicked over the keyboard with impressive speed. "I'm pleased to meet you, Mr. Blaine."

The final comment was added as an afterthought and without benefit of a glance.

Rich shuffled uncomfortably. "And you are...?"

She leaned forward, hit the backspace and re-entered a number. "Catrina Jordan."

"Catrina. That's a lovely name." He repeated her name, which was pronounced Cat-rina, emphasis on "Cat," rather than the softer European pronunciation. "Your mother must have been a feline fancier."

"My mother was allergic to cats. I was named after my grandmother." Another correction made its way to the monitor. She studied her notes a moment, then went back to inputting figures without further comment.

"I see." Rick felt like a high-school nerd trying to ask the homecoming queen for a date. "My mother was a big Humphrey Bogart fan." He flashed his famous smile, presuming she would be dazzled by it.

And she might have been, if she'd bothered to look up. "He was a fine actor."

He puffed his cheeks, blew out a breath. "She

named me after Humphrey Bogart's character in *Casablanca.*"

"How interesting," she murmured in a tone that clearly implied she'd rather discuss the genetics of animal dander with an intellectual dwarf than indulge in further conversation with him.

"Look, I want to apologize for what happened earlier. I didn't mean to embarrass you. I mean, if you were embarrassed there was no need to be. This is a casual company. We're all on pretty much a first-name basis here. It didn't occur to me that you'd be intimidated just because my name is on the letterhead."

Her fingers froze over the keyboard, then she tucked them in her lap. She took a deep breath, then swivelled around to face him. "I was not intimidated, Mr. Blaine, nor am I interested in conducting an office flirtation with the boss, or with anyone else for that matter. I take my work very seriously, and I'm good at what I do. I need this job. I'll be a valuable employee for your company, but that is all I will be."

If she'd shoved her keyboard down his throat sideways he couldn't have been more shocked. "Exactly what kind of reputation do I have among my employees?"

The dart of her gaze proved he'd hit a nerve. "You are highly regarded," she confessed. "Everyone I've spoken with thinks the world of you."

"So I'm not known as a lecherous skirt-chaser?"

That adorable flush revealed itself in crimson patches on her otherwise perfect complexion. "On the contrary, you're known as a man who is generous and outgoing to everyone."

"And you just naturally resent generous, outgoing people?"

His teasing question was rewarded by the hint of a smile, which she quickly quashed by biting her lip. "I apologize for my rudeness. The truth is that you're right, I was embarrassed because I didn't know who you were and because I'd made such a fool of myself in your presence. I presumed you were deliberately taunting me. Perhaps I was mistaken."

"Perhaps?" He tilted his head in a manner he knew was boyish and unthreatening. "Let's start over, shall we?" He stuck out his hand. "My name is Blaine, Rick Blaine. I work here."

She hesitated, then offered her hand. "Catrina Jordan. I work here too."

Her hand nested in his with a perfect fit. It was soft to the touch, a warm contrast to her cool demeanor. "I hope we can be friends, Catrina."

Apparently that was the wrong thing to say, because she withdrew her hand with more speed than would normally be expected. "I'm sure we will be, Mr. Blaine."

"Rick."

"Very well. Rick." With that, she swiveled her chair toward the monitor and began inputting figures into the computer.

Rick stood there like a spurned suitor, knowing he should muster whatever small dignity he retained by walking quickly to the nearest exit.

As usual, however, Rick rarely did what he should do, but followed his instinct instead. He took the opportunity of studying this unexpected woman, the firm curve of her jaw, the determined crease of her chin.

He'd seen fear in her eyes when she'd looked at him, a fear that both saddened and intrigued him. He acknowledged that Catrina Jordan represented a challenge, not only to his masculine ego but to his sense of humanity. Something had wounded her, something she still feared, something that she apparently recognized in him. Even though this seriously bothered him, Rick chose not to explore it too closely.

He wanted to know about this lovely young woman, wanted to know everything about her, what she enjoyed, what she disliked, what made her laugh, what brought out the joy in those luscious brown eyes.

A glance around her desk gave him a few tantalizing hints. There were no personal items, no family photographs. Her ring finger was bare, a fact he'd noticed when he'd first seen her threatening the collating machine.

He spotted a small but healthy philodendron plant at the edge of her desk, alongside an extra-large disposable cup emblazoned by the logo of a coffee boutique not far from the office. She liked plants and gourmet coffee.

On the floor behind her chair was a gym bag with a pair of running shoes tied to the handle. She was a probably a jogger, and he presumed she headed to the nearby park during lunch hour since she'd brought her fitness togs into the office.

He was still scrutinizing her personal effects when she suddenly spun around, skewered him with a stare. "Will there be anything else, Mr. Blaine?"

"Uh...nice plant."

"Thank you."

Feeling chastised and thoroughly dismissed, he backed away and returned to the spot where Frank Glasgow had been watching with obvious disapproval.

"It's not my place to question," Frank said, "but I thought you had rather firm rules against, well, mixing business with pleasure, so to speak."

"Is it that obvious?"

"I'm afraid so."

Heaving a sigh, Rick absently ran his knuckles over his scalp, a habit that made it even more difficult to control a shock of nut-brown hair that drove his barber crazy. Frank was right, of course. Rules were rules, and no business could be effective if its employees were constantly sizing each other up for romantic entanglement.

But there was something about Catrina Jordan, something that stuck like a sharp tack somewhere inside Rick's chest and wouldn't let go. "Rules are like mirrors. You never mean to break them, but sometimes it just happens."

Frank shook his head. "I hope you know what you're doing."

"So do I," Rick replied quietly. "So do I."

Chapter Two

"One large house blend, please, to go."

Pushed and prodded by the crowd around the counter, Catrina struggled to extract the cash to pay for her purchase, only to have her wallet elbowed from her grasp by a burly patron. Frustrated, she bent to retrieve it, but it was wedged under the heel of a large, booted foot. She puffed her cheeks, blew out a breath.

It was definitely going to be one of those days.

"Excuse me, sir. Sir?" She hesitated, then tugged the hem of the blue jeans extended over the offending boot. A man with a brushy beard sniffed the air like a puzzled grizzly before frowning down at her. She swallowed, tried for a smile. "You're standing on my wallet."

He blinked, glowered, stepped to one side.

Murmuring her thanks, Catrina scooped up her

wallet, gasping in horror as the coin purse yawned open to disperse a handful of jingling change.

Coins rolled across the crowded floor, lodging between a forest of shifting legs and shuffling feet, where only a desperately broke masochist would venture in an attempt to retrieve them.

Catrina dropped to her knees and frantically scooped up as many as she could find.

By the time she slapped a handful of coins on the counter along with her last dollar bill, flyaway strands of hair stuck to her moist cheek, there was a hole the size of Wyoming in the knee of her panty hose, and she was pretty sure that her deodorant had failed.

It was barely 7:30 a.m.

She shouldered her purse, snatched her covered cup of coffee, then muscled her way through the surging crowd desperately hoping that everything that could go wrong already had. Then she collided with a well-formed chest wrapped in a casual knit shirt sporting the suspiciously familiar scent of soap and cedar.

"Well, fancy meeting you here." Rick Blaine widened his eyes as if stunned by the coincidence. "Ms. Horton? Catherine, right?"

She managed a tight smile, spoke through her teeth. "Jordan, Catrina Jordan."

"Of course. I remember now." He flashed a grin, pushed the glass door open and held it for her.

She grunted her thanks and brushed by him, striding quickly up the sidewalk toward the office. She wasn't surprised when he fell into step beside her.

"I see we both have excellent taste in coffee." He

angled a speculative glance at the capped cup in her hand. "Latte, skim?"

"House blend, black."

"Ah, that explains it."

"Explains what?"

"Your rather high-strung and spirited disposition."

She swivelled to stare at him, stumbling on an uneven patch of concrete. "I beg your pardon?"

He was sipping his coffee through a small hole in the cap, and allowed himself to complete the process before favoring her with a glance. "No insult intended, of course. Anyone who starts the day with enough caffeine to jump-start a semi is bound to be a bit jittery, that's all."

"I am not jittery."

"You haven't drunk your coffee yet."

"Coffee or no coffee, I am not a jittery person." The nerve of this man, a virtual stranger presuming to cast comments upon her personality. "It's ridiculous for you to make such a categorical statement about a person you don't even know."

"You're quite right, it is. The only way for me to make reparations for my boorish presumption is to rectify that situation. How about dinner tonight?"

Only then did she note the sly gleam in his eye and realize that she'd leaped right into the trap. "No, thank you."

"Tomorrow night?"

"No. Thank you."

"Ever?"

"Probably not."

"Ah, *probably* leaves the door open."

"No, it doesn't." She reminded herself that this man had the power to take her job away, a job that she desperately needed to care for her baby daughter. "Please, don't take it personally. I'm not in the market for a romantic relationship, or any relationship for that matter."

"Not even a friendship?"

"In my experience, *friendship* is nothing more than the masculine code word for sex without commitment."

He choked on his coffee, coughed until his eyes watered. When he could speak without wheezing, he stared at her in genuine astonishment. "Don't hold back, tell me what you think."

She couldn't bite back a smile this time. He really was a charming fellow and definitely an attractive one. Under other circumstances, she would have been flattered by his attention and might even have responded favorably to it. "I apologize if I've insulted you. I do have an unfortunate tendency to speak my mind a bit too candidly at times."

"No, no, I appreciate candor." He frowned, shot her a glance. "That's a lie. I hate candor."

"Most men do."

"Most women do, too. For example, would you appreciate being told that the hole in your nylons makes you look like you have a fist-sized wart on your knee?" He grinned when she jerked to a stop and stared at him. "I didn't think so."

Her astonishment melted into amusement. She chuckled. "Touché, Mr. Blaine."

"Rick."

"Touché, Rick."

They had reached the offices of Blaine Architectural. He politely opened the door for her. "So now that we know each other well enough for brutal honesty, will you go out with me?"

"No," she said pleasantly. "But I will regret it more than I would have ten minutes ago."

"It's because of my eyebrows, isn't it?"

"Your what?"

"My eyebrows. I know they're ugly. They tweak in the middle, sag at the side, and I've been told they make me look like a stunned Chihuahua. I'll bet you hate dogs."

"I love dogs."

"Then why won't you go out with me?"

Exasperated, she stepped into the elevator, whirled around and pressed a palm in the center of his chest to keep him from following. "Because you are rich, arrogant and pushy. Does that about cover it?"

He blinked. "Yes, I believe it does."

The midday sun was warm, the autumn air cool, and the shady park was bustling with activity. From his vantage point behind a sprawling cedar, Rick watched the svelte blonde completing her warm-up exercises beside a glossy, forest-green bench. She rolled her arms, flexing her shoulders beneath a sweatsuit worn thin at the elbows, and patched at the knees. Her shoes were old too, scuffed and scarred from repeated use.

It didn't matter. She could have been wrapped in stenciled burlap, and Rick still would have thought her the most appealing woman on Earth.

He didn't know why.

Fascinated, he continued to stare as she stretched her calf muscles, dipping down until her forehead brushed her knee. Every movement was fluid and graceful, the epitome of vibrant health and lithe femininity.

His greedy gaze absorbed every nuance, every twist of her waist, every bend of her knee until she shook her body as if it were a limp rag. As soon as he realized she was preparing to sprint away, he emerged from behind the tree, planting himself directly in her view.

It took a moment for her stunned double take to announce that she'd recognized him. He pasted a grin on his face, offered a cheery wave. Even though she was at least fifty feet away, he saw her brows furrow in a suspicious frown.

Initially he'd planned to jog alongside her, try to engage her in conversation. The look in her eye made him rethink that option. Instead, he simply called out, "Nice day for a workout, isn't it?"

She simply stared at him.

Rick felt his jaw slacken. He'd never in his life had to work so hard to win a woman's interest. Nor had he ever been so determined to do so.

Clearly she was not approachable at the moment, so Rick decided to carry his charade a bit further by emulating the warm-up exercises he'd just watched her perform. Placing his hands on his hips, he twisted his upper body several times. A glance out of the corner of his eye confirmed that she was watching him. Emboldened, he flashed another of his winning smiles, then stretched out one leg as she'd done, and flung his torso forward, planning to touch his forehead to his knee.

Something popped in back.

His spine went numb. He could no longer feel the outstretched leg, and the one on which he was supporting his weight began to quiver madly.

The horror of his situation dawned on him a fraction of a second before he toppled sideways into a clumsy heap. The moment he hit the ground, his left calf went into spasms. He let out a howl, grabbed his leg, and writhed like a clumsy snake, oblivious to the startled stares of passersby.

By the time he'd kneaded the knots out of his muscles, the path beside the forest-green park bench was empty. Catrina was gone.

Rick limped back to the office, daunted but determined. Whether Catrina Jordan realized it or not, she'd thrown down a gauntlet of challenge.

Pain shot from his lower back to his shoulder blades. Rick sucked a breath, listening to the shower sounds emanating from the women's locker room. He'd guessed that she'd use the health club on the top floor of their office building to change clothes and shower after her lunchtime jog, and the familiar battered duffel left on one of the workout benches confirmed his assumption.

He also presumed that she had witnessed his clumsy tumble in the park and had no doubt been mightily amused by it. Ego wouldn't allow him to let her believe that he was inept enough to have actually hurt himself, so he'd dragged himself up here to put on yet another show of machismo.

She would no doubt appreciate the effort. Women always appreciated a cunning display of male physical prowess. And Rick appreciated their appreciation. Even if it was undeserved.

Slowly, painfully, he lowered himself onto a weight bench, which supported his torso as he planted his feet on the floor. A tubular rack above his head held an iron bar affixed to a set of iron discs. The past ten years had not been the most athletic of his life, but in college Rick could bench press one hundred pounds without breaking a sweat, so it didn't occur to him to double-check the weight of the unit. Besides, he didn't want to move again until he absolutely had to. A lack of routine exercise was revealed in the tremor of his strained muscles.

He was already panting like a whipped dog, his back was killing him, but the sound of running water in the women's locker room had just been replaced by the whir of a hair dryer so it was nearly show time.

He sucked a breath, curled his fingers around the bar over his head and waited.

Within a matter of minutes, Catrina emerged from the locker room wearing street clothes, and carrying her jogging ensemble under her arm. He noticed that her ruined nylons had been removed, leaving her legs bare and pale and exquisitely attractive.

She didn't spare him a glance. Instead she stuffed her sweatsuit into the open duffel, grabbed her worn-out shoes from beneath the bench and tied them to the bag handle.

She was clearly preoccupied. Her lips pursed in a sensual pout, her pale brows puckered with appealing concentration. Her skin was slightly flushed from the shower, a pink glow from cheek to jaw that imparted an appealing radiance to her creamy complexion.

Rick thought she was just about the most beautiful woman he'd ever seen in his life.

He cleared his throat. "Hello, again."

She spun around, touched her throat in a gesture of vulnerability that he found strangely enticing.

"Our paths just keep crossing." He flexed his fingers around the weight bar, fought a grimace as his back issued a protest. "Uncanny, isn't it?"

Tilting her head, she regarded him. "Yes, uncanny."

"I would have joined you at the park, but I didn't want you to feel bad if you couldn't keep up."

She smiled then, a brief flutter of lips that was absolutely devastating. "I'm sure you would have left me in the dust. Presuming, of course, you had stayed on your feet in the first place."

Well, at least she'd been watching him. He took some small consolation in that. "A minor mishap. Have you never gotten a pebble in your shoe?"

"A pebble?"

"Sharp little devil. Poked itself right into my instep. You know how it goes."

A flash of tooth scraped her lower lip, as if she was biting back a smile. "Of course."

"So other than jogging, what else do you do to buff up?"

"'Buff up'?"

"You know, tone the old quads, beef up the biceps."

"Oh. Well, I enjoy tennis. Or I used to. There's little time for it any more."

A clue. He pounced on it. "This is truly amazing. Tennis is absolutely my game." Grab a ball, hit it with a racket. How hard could it be? "Maybe we could share a court some time."

"Maybe."

She was softening, he could see it in her eyes. "You ought to try working with the weights, too. It's great for the cardiovascular system." To prove the point, he hoisted the bar with a macho grunt and felt something give at the base of his spine. His arms collapsed like wet noodles, and the bar came down on his chest, pushing the air out of his lungs with a humiliating whoosh.

Catrina widened her eyes. "Are you all right?"

He opened his mouth, sucked a wheezing breath. "I meant..." a peculiar hiss emanating from somewhere deep inside "...to do that."

She blinked. "Why?"

It took a few seconds before he could speak again. "Lower weights—" he wheezed "—then lift them." He wheezed again. "That's how...it works."

"I see," she murmured, clearly unconvinced. "Well, I'll leave you to your workout."

Rick smiled, managed a painful nod. "If you see Frank Glasgow, could you...send him up?"

"Of course." She glanced once more in his direction, then scooped up her duffel and left.

After what seemed a small eternity, Frank poked his head into the gym. "What can I do for you?"

"You can get this...damned thing off." Rick gritted his teeth. "Then drive me to the hospital... I think I broke a rib."

"I tell you, Gracie, it's absolutely eerie. Every time I turn around, there he is. And he's sending me presents."

"Presents?" Gracie's eyes popped. "You mean like diamonds and perfume and furs?"

"Well, no." Catrina cleared her throat, glanced away. "Er, a case of panty hose." Expensive panty hose, attached to a dozen colorful helium-filled balloons and shuttled to her apartment door by a uniformed courier who was most unhappy when she refused to accept the delivery.

Gracie blinked rapidly. "Oh, my, that does sound a bit personal."

"Actually, it was kind of a private joke. You see, I dropped some coins at the coffee shop and ripped the knee out of my—" Blushing furiously, Catrina clamped her mouth shut, embarrassed by Gracie's knowing grin. "Never mind. The point is, I think he's stalking me."

"Stalking you?" Gracie chuckled. "Perhaps he's just interested in you. After all, you're a very attractive young lady."

"Well, I'm not interested in him."

She quirked a brow. "Not even a little?"

Catrina shrugged, shifted Heather on her hip as she tossed a handful of pasta into a pot of boiling water. "I'll admit he's an appealing man, but that isn't the point. I'm not interested in any man, appealing or not."

"You prefer women?"

"Gracie!" Catrina laughed, shook her head. "You know what I mean. I've just extricated myself from one bad relationship. I certainly am not going to fling myself into another one."

"Then how about flinging yourself into a good relationship?"

Catrina's smile faded. "There's no such thing," she said firmly, and meant it. "My mother suffered through two terrible marriages. Two men used her, abused her then walked out on her. My eldest sister divorced a man so shallow and narcissistic that he ran off to Europe rather than support the child he had fathered, and I ended up with a fellow who thought women should have been born with scrub brushes instead of fingers, and a built-in beer cooler on their backs. Heather and I are better off alone, thank you very much."

"Not all men are adolescent control freaks."

"Of course not. Just the ones I know." Sighing, she slipped Heather into the high chair, handing her a spouted cup of juice to placate her until dinner was ready. "I understand that it's not fair to judge an entire gender by the behavior of a few, but the point is that I can't afford another mistake. I have a child to think about, a child who means the world to me. I won't risk having her hurt, her trust broken by yet another daddy who will disappoint and abandon her."

"There are good men out there, Catrina, men who are worthy of your love and respect."

A slow throb worked its way around her temples. "Then why couldn't you find one?" The minute the words emerged, Catrina regretted them. "I'm sorry. I didn't mean—"

"Of course you did." Paling visibly, Gracie nonetheless attempted a smile. "I'm the first to admit that when it came to choosing husbands, I wasn't the brightest porch light on the block."

"Gracie—"

"No, no, you're right. I'm hardly an authority on relationships." She shifted her gaze, stirred the pot of spaghetti sauce bubbling on Catrina's stove. "Just because you invite me for dinner once a week doesn't give me license to tell you how to live your life." A sly glance bounced so quickly that Catrina nearly missed it. "I'm sure you're not the least bit interested in my silly musings."

"Of course I'm interested," Catrina assured her. "If I didn't want your opinion, I wouldn't have brought the subject up in the first place."

Gracie laid the saucy spoon on the counter, wiped her hands on a tea towel. "Are you sure?"

"Yes, I'm sure."

"I wouldn't want to intrude—"

"Gracie! Tell me what you think I should do."

The older woman's face spread into a wreath of smile lines. "Well, since you've asked, I think you should continue doing exactly what you've been doing."

"I've been ignoring and avoiding him."

"Exactly."

Catrina frowned. For some reason, she'd had the impression that Gracie thought she should give the persistent Rick Blaine a chance. "So far, it hasn't exactly chilled his enthusiasm."

"Give it time. Just keep pretending you're not interested and—"

"*Pretending?* Gracie, I don't have to pretend. Haven't you been listening? I am not interested in Rick Blaine. Not, not, not!"

"Of course, dear, I understand." The woman chuckled, swished her hand as if waving away a pesky fly. "Anyway, you just keep doing exactly what you've been doing, and sooner or later you'll get exactly what you want."

"Exactly what I want," Catrina repeated. The words rolled around her tongue with a smooth feel, a unique flavor. "That would be lovely, of course, if I knew what I wanted in the first place. The truth is I haven't a clue. Does that make me insane?"

"No dear," Gracie said with a chuckle. "It simply makes you human."

Chapter Three

"It's about time you answered. I've been calling for two hours." Rick shifted the tiny cell phone, touched the brake and cruised to a stop at the light. "You missed a terrific steak dinner."

"I wasn't aware we had a date."

"We didn't, but we would have if you'd answered your phone two hours ago."

The familiar feminine chuckle on the other end of the line never ceased to make him smile. "I suppose I should be flattered that a handsome scalawag like yourself would waste a perfectly good Friday night on an old woman."

"You are not old. You have simply blossomed fully."

"Such a silver-tongued lad! No wonder you have to beat women off with a stick." Her chuckle rolled into a tinkling laugh that warmed him from nape to spine. "I'm thinking you must have whacked a tad too hard if you've a free weekend. Either that or the young woman at the office who has taken your fancy must not be as easily persuaded by your charms as you'd hoped."

"Can't a fellow hold a Friday night open for a date with his favorite Mom without being taunted and abused?"

"She turned you down, did she?"

"Not at all." An impatient honk from behind startled him. He touched the accelerator to join the thrumming rush of vehicles across the intersection. "I'm sure if I'd invited her to dinner, she'd have leaped at the opportunity."

A gleeful whoop made him grimace. "Aha! She slammed the door in your face, didn't she?"

"Not literally." Although Rick had little doubt that if he'd had the chutzpah to appear on her porch, the seemingly unattainable and undeniably gorgeous Catrina Jordan would have done just that. "The subject never came up, that's all."

"Yes, well it's difficult to ask someone out on a date if they won't give you the time of day to begin with."

Rick found himself giving the cell phone a wry stare. "Thank you for the maternal support and encouragement."

"Why should I encourage you to break another woman's heart?"

The allegation stunned him. "I've never broken any woman's heart. Every woman I've ever dated has become a lifelong friend."

"Your charm is both a curse and a blessing, dear. People are drawn to you like a magnet, but just as one side attracts, the other propels those who would move too close a safe distance away." Her sigh was poignant, heavy with a sadness that Rick understood, although he wished he didn't. "It seems that we always most desperately want that which we cannot have."

"Mom, please. Don't start."

"Don't start on what? The fact that I will be laid in my grave without a grandchild to grieve my passing?"

He whipped the steering wheel, pulled into a drive that sloped sharply below street level, and stopped at a striped gate. "We've been over this before."

"Yes, we have. Tell me again why the very thought of marriage and family makes you break into a cold sweat."

"You know why." He pressed a button on the armrest with more force than necessary. The window slid down, allowing him to slide the parking-garage access card through the reader. He hated this conversation. He'd always hated it. "I'm flying up to Tahoe next week to talk to a man about renovating a casino. How about joining me? You've never met a slot machine you didn't like, and I promise to keep a never-ending supply of quarters handy—"

"You are thirty-six years old, Rick. It's time you settled down."

"Mom—"

"I want grandchildren!"

"Then rent some." Regretting the snap of his tone, Rick sighed, eased his vehicle into his parking space and shoved the transmission into park. "Mom, please. Trust me when I say that I am doing the females of the world a favor by removing myself from the marriage pool."

Her voice softened. "Don't let my failures harden you."

"You didn't fail. They did."

She sighed, a whisper of disappointment that stirred something deep inside Rick's soul. It was the sigh of a woman scarred by pain, wounded by betrayals that she refused to acknowledge. But Rick acknowledged them, those traitorous emotions that had blinded his beloved mother to the cruelty of misplaced trust. After all the hurt, all the pain, she still viewed life through an optimistic aura of hope, the staunch belief that there was no pain so intense that it couldn't be eased with love and chicken soup.

As much as Rick adored his mother, he saw in her the same cynical naïveté that he'd recognized in Catrina Jordan's eyes, eyes that reflected past pain and betrayal, yet still sparked with wounded vulnerability and a silent hope that had touched a chord deep inside him.

He didn't know why he'd felt such instant kinship, such intense desire to nurture and protect. He didn't know why her image haunted his thoughts, why her scent floated through his dreams. It was as if he had suddenly discovered a lost part of himself, an appendage of his soul that had been missing for so long he'd forgotten it ever existed.

"Rick, are you still there?"

"It's late," he whispered. "You should get some rest."

"I suppose so."

"Mom?"

"Yes?"

He paused. "I love you."

"I love you, too, dear. Good night."

A soft click, a crackle of static and she was gone.

Darkness shrouded him in the dim parking bunker. An eerie concrete coldness enveloped him. It was, he thought, like being entombed in a vehicle graveyard, surrounded by idle hulks of steel that had been tossed aside and forgotten until they could once again be useful.

The analogy was strangely unsettling.

It was a discomfiting mirror of his own life, a life he reflected upon only during times like this, times when he was completely alone, undistracted by the comfortable chatter and bustle of people with which he deliberately surrounded himself.

Quietly alone. Silently alone.

Alone.

Panic crept softly, slithering through the shadows of his mind, chilling the unlit corners of his soul. Loneliness was a dark destiny, but Rick accepted it. There was no other choice.

Frowning, Frank Glasgow stepped off the elevator, clasping his hands behind his back. He took two steps into the hallway, then spun to glower at Catrina. "Surely you were informed that certain training sessions would be required."

"Yes, of course—"

"Then it's settled." Pivoting sharply, he strode toward the warren of executive offices at the north side of the floor.

Catrina hurried after him, feeling frantic. "But a

two-day seminar halfway across the state? Even if I could afford the travel cost, I can't possibly leave my daughter for that length of time."

"The company will cover your expenses. See Martha for your airline tickets and travel itinerary—" Glasgow stuttered to a stop. He swiveled his head, hiked his eyebrow. "Your daughter? You have a child?"

"Ah...yes. Is that a problem?"

"Not for me. For others, perhaps." He chuckled as if enjoying a private joke, then regarded her with undisguised amusement. "I empathize with the inconvenience. However, this fiscal programming class is a requirement of the position. Surely you must have been informed of that fact during your pre-employment processing?"

She shifted, licked her lips. "Yes, but I didn't understand that it would require being out of town for several days."

"Is there no one who can care for the child while you're gone?"

"I'm afraid not."

His amusement faded into annoyance. "You're a fine accounting clerk, Ms. Jordan. We'll be sorry to lose you."

It took a moment for the impact of his words to sink in. "You'd actually fire me because I can't find a babysitter?"

"Of course not." Glasgow spoke slowly, succinctly, with the exaggerated pronunciation one uses with animals and small children. "You will, however, be terminated if you are unable to fulfill the requirements of your job. As previously explained, this training seminar is such a requirement."

"But my daughter—"

"—is your responsibility," he snapped. "There are many single parents in our employ. We make accommodations when possible, but we will not sacrifice the quality of our work to do so. Is that understood?"

Catrina swallowed hard. "Yes, sir. Understood."

With a curt nod, Glasgow turned on his heel and marched into one of the spacious offices lining the executive hallway.

Exhaling all at once, Catrina sagged against a wall and fought a surge of sheer panic. She needed this job desperately, but the thought of leaving Heather for three days...well, it wasn't even a consideration. Having been in Los Angeles only a few months, Catrina didn't know anyone in Los Angeles well enough to trust them to care for her child. Except for Gracie Appleby, of course. But asking a busy businesswoman in her sixties to chase after an exuberant toddler for that length of time certainly went above and beyond the call of friendship.

"Don't worry about Frank."

A cheerful feminine voice startled her. She spun around to see an attractive brunette with chocolate-brown eyes and a generous, grinning mouth. Catrina recognized her only as one of the apprentice designers from the architectural department.

"He truly doesn't mean to be such a grumpy stick-in-the-mud. It just happens accidentally—" the woman lowered her voice to a covert whisper

"—whenever he opens his mouth."

Catrina smiled. "Actually, Mr. Glasgow has always been quite nice to me. I understand his position."

"You mean the missionary position? Because that's the only one I can picture that unimaginative, stodgy old fart using."

The woman pitched back her head and issued a sharp, healthy burst of laughter so infectious that Catrina couldn't help but smile.

"Forgive me," she said between chuckles. "I'm crass and vulgar. I admit it. But since Frank is my father-in-law, I figure I'm entitled to an affectionate familial taunt now and again." The woman stuck out her hand. "Sandy Glasgow, at your service. You're the new kid in accounting, right?"

"Yes, Catrina Jordan."

"Nice to meet you." Sandy's handshake was warm, firm, and friendly. "I couldn't help but overhear your problem, primarily because I was eavesdropping shamelessly. How old is your baby?"

"Heather is twenty-six months old."

"Ah, the wonder years. The terrible two's." She shuddered. "My son grew horns at that age and didn't turn human again until he was ready for kindergarten."

Catrina laughed. "Well, she hasn't sprouted bony appendages from her skull, but she's certainly a handful."

"I hear you." She pursed her lips. "That training seminar is boring as hell, but it really is required for all employees. Our company uses a specialized and very complex software system that integrates 3-D graphic design with accounting and fiscal functions. There are only a couple of dozen firms that use it, so the seminars are scattered across the country. You're lucky this next one is in the state. I had to fly to Vermont.'' She tilted her head, regarded Catrina sympathetically. ''Isn't there anyone that can help you out for a few days?''

''Well, there's one person, but I couldn't possibly impose.''

Sandy shrugged. ''I could give you the names of a couple of child-care professionals, if you want. They don't come cheap, though.''

Stifling a wince, Catrina maintained what she hoped was a grateful expression. ''That's kind of you.''

It wasn't so much the cost that upset her, although heaven knew she hadn't been on the job long enough to save two dimes to rub together. It was the mere thought of leaving Heather with a total stranger that made the hairs on her nape prickle.

''No problem,'' Sandy replied. ''I'll hunt up the phone numbers, and leave them on your voicemail.''

''Thank you. I'll…'' Catrina's voice trailed off as the door to the office at the end of the hallway opened, and Rick Blaine emerged with a smiling young woman who looked happy enough to float on thin air.

The young woman was chattering madly, a voice the sound of light tinkling bells chiming so quickly that the melody was discernable, even if the individual notes were not. She was breathless, annoyingly so. And Rick Blaine was gazing down at her as if she were the most exquisite creature on the face of the earth.

A pain shot straight through Catrina's rib cage and lodged itself below her windpipe. For a brief but terrifying moment, she was overwhelmed by a surge of something so powerful it scared her half to death. She wanted to grab the laughing young lady by the scruff of her neck, boot her into the elevator and send her straight to the basement.

"You'll what?"

"Hmm?" It took a tap on her shoulder to realize that Sandy was waiting for Catrina to finish her sentence. "Oh. I, ah, I..." Her gaze shot sideways in time to see the brazen hussy fling herself into Rick Blaine's arms.

A lump of pure misery wedged in Catrina's throat. This time she recognized the ragged emotion gnawing from the inside out. It was sheer, unabashed jealousy. The realization startled her.

"I can't thank you enough!" the young woman purred, as her greedy arms captured her willing prey. "It was the most wonderful gift imaginable. I don't know how I can ever repay you."

Yeah, right, Catrina thought, and was stunned by a sudden burst of bitterness. Jealousy was not something Catrina had much experience with, particularly where it concerned a man in whom she had absolutely no proprietary interest. Of course, he was attractive. Some might even say he was gorgeous, with his flashing rogue grin and that tousled mane of coffee-brown hair that always looked as if he'd just rolled out of bed. And yes, those incredibly lush lashes added to the sensuality of his eyes, so piercing they seemed to penetrate a woman's very soul. But having noticed these obvious physical attributes certainly didn't mean Catrina had any personal interest in the man. In fact, she'd even complained to Gracie that she felt as if he'd been stalking her.

So why on Earth did she feel like strangling a woman she'd never even seen before simply because she was wrapping herself around him?

Rick made no effort to disentangle himself. "It was my pleasure."

I'll bet it was.

The thought flitted through Catrina's mind with a wry anger that startled her. A stinging in her palms was a clue that she'd balled her fists so tightly that her fingernails had scored her skin. This wasn't like her, wasn't like her at all. She didn't understand what distressed her more, the tawdry scene she was witnessing or her completely uncalled-for reaction to it.

Behind her, Sandy whispered with undisguised amusement, "Santa strikes again."

With some effort, Catrina unfurled her fingers. "I take it that Mr. Blaine has a history of offering gifts to pretty young women?"

For a moment Sandy's eyes widened in surprise, then a knowing grin spread across her face. "I keep forgetting that you're new here. Just to clue you in, our esteemed boss has a history of offering gifts to just about everyone. He's the most generous man I know, although the amateur shrinks in the office opine that he's trying to make up for an impoverished youth, or is feeding a secret insecurity of some sort." A derisive snort clearly indicated what she thought of that theory. "As if a man with shoulders like that had anything to be insecure about."

Since Catrina didn't know what to say, she said nothing at all, which was just as well since the young woman who'd just had a stranglehold on Rick's neck was bustling past, grinning as if she'd just licked the last drop of cream from a saucer.

"That's Ivana Trenton," Sandy whispered as the woman stepped into the elevator. "Her son's new bicycle was stolen from the school playground last week. She was devastated because it had been a birthday present, and with her husband out of work there was no way they could afford to replace it."

"So Mr. Blaine bought the child another one?"

"That's the rumor."

"Oh." If embarrassment were neon, Catrina would have glowed. The discovery that Rick showered just about everyone who crossed his path with the same attentive generosity he'd shown Catrina was humbling, to say the least.

So much for her suspicion that a gift of panty hose was the sinister plot by a conniving playboy hoping to gain intimate access to said garments in the future.

Even as her cheeks burned, her gaze followed his every move. From her vantage point down the carpeted hallway, Catrina watched the flick of his ivory-cuffed wrist as he adjusted his tie, smoothed tailored lapels mussed by the exuberant Ms. Trenton's gratitude.

A hint of embarrassment flickered in his eyes as he angled a glance toward his administrative assistant, whose gaze was glued to her computer monitor as her fingers clicked the keyboard. He seemed relieved that the small scene outside his office door had apparently escaped her notice.

Catrina's presence had also escaped his notice, allowing her to scrutinize him with encyclopedic detail. A muscle vibrated along his jaw as his gaze swept the executive foyer, from the busy reception desk to the row of desks tastefully arranged so that each occupant had a pleasant window view. His own gaze wandered beyond the work space, fixing somewhere in the distance, and glazing with a peculiar longing, as if he wished to be somewhere, anywhere, except the spot where he now stood.

It was an intimate glimpse into his private thought, a peek into his soul that touched Catrina deeply. Although she didn't know him well enough to decipher his expression accurately, she intuitively realized that she'd witnessed a rare lapse of emotional armor, and was drawn by the flicker of vulnerability she'd perceived.

Before she could process this dichotomy of information, Sandy's rough whisper broke into her thoughts. "He's a serious hottie, isn't he?"

"Hmm?" It took a moment before Catrina trusted her voice. "He's a striking man, yes."

A knowing smile offset the worry in Sandy's eyes. "He's every woman's Prince Charming, the stuff dreams are made of. He's also completely unavailable, so don't even think about it."

The statement took Catrina by surprise. "Think about what?"

"Don't make me spell it out," she replied, not unkindly. "I'm not blind, and I'm not stupid. The looks you've been giving him could turn ice to steam." She laid a friendly hand on Catrina's shoulder. "Rick treats every woman he meets as if she's made of glass and gold, the sun rises on her right shoulder and the moon rises on her left. He makes everyone feel special and is the most generous and charming man I've ever met. But he's also heartbreak on a stick, hon. Definitely not the marrying kind. Never has been, never will be."

When Catrina was able to hoist her jaw off the floor, she hoped her astonishment was reflected in her incredulous stare. "I cannot imagine why you felt compelled to issue that warning, since marriage to anyone, charming or not, holds about the same appeal as piercing my tongue with rusty hairpins."

Sandy widened her eyes, her lips curving into a flashing grin of honest amusement. "In that case, you might let the rest of your body know, because honey, I'm here to tell you that you were staring at Rick Blaine the way a starving man eyes prime rib through a restaurant window."

Before Catrina could sputter an indignant denial, Sandy slipped a glance past her shoulder, and whispered, "Wipe the drool off your chin, hon. Here comes the main course."

A prickling warmth down her spine had already issued that warning. Catrina didn't have to turn around to know that the subject of their conversation was standing close behind her.

"Hey, Rick," Sandy said with admirable aplomb. "I heard the Melbourne contract is in the bag. Congratulations."

"Congratulate Frank," came the smooth reply. "He laid all the groundwork."

"I'll tell him you said so." Sandy slipped Catrina a smile that was clearly an admonition. "Remember what we talked about, hon. I'll catch you later."

With that she slipped into the open elevator and was still smiling when the doors closed.

Courtesy dictated that Catrina turn around and acknowledge the man hovering close enough that she was dizzied by his scent. For some reason, she feared doing so, feared that he'd note the same secret yearning in her eyes that Sandy had so astutely recognized.

Not since her adolescence, when she'd swooned over a poster of some now-forgotten buff teen idol, had she felt so utterly entranced and infatuated. And she didn't have a clue why.

All her life men had disappointed and abandoned her. She must be a masochist to allow yet another one to stir those long-suppressed feelings. So she wouldn't allow it.

Straightening her shoulders, she arranged her features into an expression of pleasant neutrality and turned to face him. "Good afternoon, Mr. Blaine—"

"Rick." His smile nearly melted her kneecaps. "We don't rest on formalities around here, remember?"

"Of course." She hoped the stiff stretching of her mouth bore some resemblance to a smile. "Rick."

He shifted, tucked his hands in his slacks pockets. If she didn't know better, she'd think he was nervous. "So how are things going for you?"

"Fine, thank you."

"How do you like your job?"

"Very much. It's challenging, but quite rewarding."

"Good, good." He rocked back on his heels, glanced around the hallway as if noticing a framed seascape for the first time. For a moment Catrina thought he would comment on the painting. Instead, he stunned her. "I owe you an apology."

"An apology?"

"Yes." His jaw twitched. He didn't make eye contact, which was unusual for him because Catrina's covert observations had revealed that he scrupulously studied each person to whom he spoke with meticulous attention. "It only occurred to me after you returned my gift that you might have considered it...inappropriate."

A slow heat warmed her jawline. "Oh, that."

"I truly meant no offense. I thought you'd be amused." He nodded a greeting to a pair of gray-suited executives who passed by, then coughed lightly into his fist. "I mean, under the circumstances of our meeting in the coffee shop, and the untimely demise of...ah, well, you know."

"Yes, I know." Her smile relaxed as she recalled crawling around the floor like a desperate cockroach, scooping up spilled coins and scouring holes in the knees of her nylons. "You've witnessed more than one of my least graceful moments."

"We all have our share of those."

"I suppose." She doubted this perfect figure of a man had ever had such a lapse of decorum, beyond that amusing little tumble in the park. Although the way he continued to avoid her gaze while nervously fingering his necktie did seem oddly out of character for a man supposedly so self-assured about the power of his own charm. "I didn't mean returning them to be an insult. The gift took me by surprise, that's all. I hadn't realized that you were generous with all of your employees."

His wandering gaze slipped to hers, capturing her like a vice. She couldn't have looked away if she'd wanted to. "I enjoy pleasing people, if that's what you mean."

"Of course," she murmured, wondering if she'd inadvertently touched a raw nerve.

"Did you think I was trying to seduce you?"

The candor of the question knocked her back a step. She felt her face flame with the truth. That was exactly what she'd thought. But what truly embarrassed her was the disappointing realization that it hadn't been true. "I simply didn't understand the close relationship you establish with all of your employees."

"So the next time I send you a gift, you will accept?"

She swallowed hard, tried to pry her gaze from his, only to feel helplessly pinned by those haunting blue eyes. "Actually, I'd prefer that there wasn't a next time."

"It makes you uncomfortable?"

"Yes."

"Good." He smiled at her expression. "That means that I make you uncomfortable. I like that."

"Why?"

His voice lowered to a seductive murmur. "Because you make me uncomfortable too, Catrina Jordan. And I intend to find out why."

With that, he offered a wicked smile, a gentlemanly nod, and before Catrina could close her gaping mouth, he disappeared into his office, closing the door behind him.

Chapter Four

"Yes, I know the center closes at six, but there must be some way to make arrangements for overnight care." Clamping the cordless phone between her chin and shoulder, Catrina shifted her cranky toddler in the crook of her arm. "Shh, sweetie," she whispered. "Mommy needs to talk for just a few more minutes, okay?"

Heather rubbed her wet eyes, sniffed and wriggled impatiently. "Want cookie!"

"I know—" A voice from the phone captured Catrina's attention. "I'm sorry, what did you say?"

The voice took on a long-suffering tone. "I said that our day-care center is just that, day care only. We have no arrangements for overnight care. I'm sorry."

Not as sorry as Catrina was. Before she could respond, Heather arched her back, squirming, and nearly bucked out of her arms.

"Want cookie!"

"Just a few more—" As she tightened her grasp, the phone slipped from beneath her chin and fell to the floor.

And the doorbell rang.

Groaning, Catrina shifted the squirming baby, yanked the door open with her free hand, and was scooping the phone off the floor when Gracie sauntered in carrying a rented videotape.

Catrina managed a harried smile of welcome and would have returned to her phone conversation had Heather not lurched out of her arms shrieking, "Gamma Gacie, Gamma Gacie!!"

Gracie chuckled, held out her hands. The gleeful toddler threw herself into the older woman's embrace. "And how's my precious girl today, hmm?"

"Want cookie, Gamma."

"A cookie, is it?" Grace hiked a brow, angling a questioning glance at Catrina, who managed a tired nod. "Well, then, a cookie it shall be. Let's see what's in the cupboard, shall we?"

Squealing happily, Heather clapped her pudgy hands as Gracie carried her into the kitchen, allowing Catrina to finish her phone conversation.

Unfortunately, it was already just about finished. "So the center doesn't have a list of qualified individuals who might be willing to—"

"I'm afraid not."

"There are no child-care professionals that you could recommend?"

"No, I'm sorry," came the bored reply. "You might try a nanny service."

"A nanny service?" Catrina's heart sank like a

rock. "I couldn't possibly afford that. Besides, I'm not looking for live-in help, just someone to watch my daughter for a couple of days."

"I don't know what else to tell you."

"I see. Well, thank you for your time." Pivoting the phone in her palm, she clicked it off with her thumb and tossed it onto a nearby table. "Rats."

Gracie emerged from the cramped apartment kitchen, carrying Heather, happily munching a sugar cookie. "Problems, dear?"

"Hmm? Oh, nothing important." She pasted on a cheery smile, rubbed her hands together. Once a week Gracie came over for an evening of Mel Gibson movies and girl talk. "Okay, I'll start the popcorn. What juicy morsel have you scrounged up at the video store for tonight's entertainment fest?"

"Don't change the subject. I'm already insulted."

"Insulted?"

"Yes, insulted." She put the toddler down, then faced Catrina with her hands on her hips and a frown on her face. "What's this about trying to hire strangers to care for my unofficially adopted grandbaby?"

Catrina smiled. It truly was a crime that Gracie, who adored children with every fiber of her being, had no grandchildren, while Heather's own grandparents wanted nothing to do with her simply because Catrina's blood ran in her veins. "I'm being sent out of town for a couple of days, some kind of mandatory software training seminar."

"Oh? Sounds interesting. Why haven't you mentioned it before?"

"I just found out yesterday. Besides, I didn't want—" Clearing her throat, she averted her gaze.

"I didn't want you to feel obligated to volunteer, which is what you're about to do, isn't it?"

"Of course. Do you honestly think I'd sit back and let a total stranger care for this precious child?"

"Gracie, you are so special. I don't know what I'd do without your friendship." Catrina sighed. "But I can't continue to impose on you that way. You have a business to run. A rambunctious toddler squealing around the bookcases for two hours is one thing. Two days, closer to three days with the travel time involved, is an entirely different matter. She'd drive you insane."

"Nonsense. I can't think of anything that would give me greater joy. Besides, I've been looking for a scheme to get you out of the way for a while so Heather and I can spend some quality time together. The matter is settled."

"Gracie—"

Gracie quelled her with a look. "Unless, of course, you don't trust me to care for your daughter."

Catrina sighed. "There is no one on Earth I trust more," she said honestly. "It's just that I'm always taking advantage of you, of our friendship. You have given so much, and I have so little to offer in return."

For a moment, a peculiar light emanated from the woman's crisp, blue eyes, a softness that was both touching and poignant. "Oh, child. You have no idea how much you have offered, and the tremendous joy with which I've accepted the gift." She inhaled deeply, sending an indulgent smile at the baby toddling across the floor with wet cookie crumbs smeared over her fat face. "In the few weeks since you and Heather first entered my bookstore, my life has been truly blessed."

A lump wedged in Catrina's throat, rendering her momentarily mute.

Gracie glanced up, her smile fading into concern. "What is it, dear? You look like you're about to cry."

"I...am." She swallowed, dabbed her moist eyes. "I just realized how very long it's been since anyone cherished us, actually enjoyed our presence rather than merely tolerated it."

"You deserve to be cherished, Catrina, both of you. You deserve to be loved. Someday I hope you'll learn to believe that." A warm silence spread between them, broken only when Gracie cleared her throat. "Well. Speaking of such romantic notions, how are things going with that young man of yours?"

"I have no man, Gracie, young or otherwise." She flushed, turned away, busied herself straightening the mail she'd scattered across the dining-room table. "If you're referring to the enigmatic Mr. Blaine and his inappropriate gift of intimate apparel, it seems that I've mistaken his intentions."

"Oh?" The word was soft, deceptively neutral, although the woman's eyes shone with interest.

Catrina shrugged, embarrassed to recall the egotistical presumption that a man like Rick Blaine had been, or could ever be, romantically attracted to a harried, nearly bankrupt single mom. "I, ah, misunderstood his meaning."

"Did you now?"

"Umm." Anxious to change the subject, Catrina's

gaze slipped to the rectangular videotape Gracie had brought. "So, what's tonight's offering? Mel chasing bad guys, Mel on a motorcycle, Mel fighting futuristic mutants, Mel in love, Mel in lust—?"

"What makes you think you've misunderstood the man's motives, Catrina? It seems to me that he's made his intentions quite clear. A man does not pursue a woman he's not interested in, nor does he shower her with gifts."

"This one does. I've found out that he's just one of those special individuals who passes presents out like candy and treats everyone he meets as if he or she is the most important person on Earth. Besides, a case of panty hose is not exactly a shower of—" She moaned as the doorbell rang again. Pivoting in annoyance, she crossed the room, yanked the door open, and was stunned to see nothing but a pair of trousered legs extending beneath the largest bouquet of red roses she'd ever seen in her life.

A muffled voice emanated from behind the massive bouquet. "Ms. Catrina Jordan?"

"Ah...yes." The roses were thrust into her arms before the final word was out of her mouth.

"Have a nice evening," the deliveryman muttered, and strode away before she could tip him.

Gracie was beside her in a heartbeat, snatching the petite envelope from a plastic prong tucked into the foliage. "Ooooh, roses. How enchanting. Dare I guess who they might be from?"

Catrina slid her a wry glance. "Why guess? Just read me the card, since you've already ripped the envelope open."

"Since you insist." Grinning, Gracie reached into

her slacks' pocket for her eyeglasses, whipping them into place with practiced efficiency. "'Forgiveness is humbly requested. How about dinner Friday night?' Signed, 'Rick'" Gracie chortled. "Well, you are quite right. This is certainly not a man who is romantically attracted to you. I'm sure he sends two dozen red roses to every woman in the office on a weekly basis."

Catrina snatched the card from Gracie's hand. "Very amusing." Despite forcing a bland expression, Catrina's heart still leapt when she touched the card. He had touched the same card, touched it with Catrina's image in his mind.

Or perhaps he simply dictated it to some harassed order clerk over the phone.

She turned the card in her palm, her pulse racing as she recognized his signature. "This doesn't mean anything," she whispered, then flushed to realize she'd spoken aloud.

Gracie set the vase on the table, sniffed one of the velvety blooms. "Mmm, how delightfully fragrant. Tell me again why this man isn't interested in you?"

It took a moment to rein in her own surge of emotion. "He's just an impulsive and generous person, Gracie. I'm sure if I checked with his personal assistant I'd learn that he sent a half-dozen bouquets this week alone, commemorating everything from a mail clerk's birthday to the bar mitzvah of an executive's son. It's just the kind of thing he does without a second thought, that's all."

"He sounds like a wonderful young man."

"He is." The words slipped out on a sigh, which she instantly swallowed, although not before Gracie's grin widened. "I mean, he seems to be. I barely know him."

"A situation he seems determined to rectify."

Her spine prickled with a cold chill. "He could be Prince Charming incarnate, Gracie, and it wouldn't matter. I don't want another man in my life. I don't want the pain they inevitably bring when they leave."

Gracie's smile faded. "They don't always leave, child. I know that with two bad marriages behind me I'm not one to talk, but you can't judge the entire world by a couple of learning experiences."

"Learning experiences? Is that what you call betrayal and abandonment?"

"Everything in life is a learning experience, dear, even that which we cannot control. I know your father left you. I know your ex-husband was a man unworthy of your love. That doesn't mean that all men are cads."

"I know that. But frankly, I'm too tired to sort through the barrel and too frightened of getting another rotten apple. I don't need the aggravation, Gracie, and my daughter certainly doesn't need the grief of watching the daddy she loves walk out the door without so much as a fond farewell."

"She's already experienced that, has she not?"

"She was only a few weeks old when her father walked out. Too young to understand or remember what was happening to her I'm thankful to say."

"*You* remember."

"I was three when my father left." Catrina turned away. She'd only been a few months older than Heather was now, and still the pain was vividly etched on her heart. "I don't want my daughter to be hurt."

"As you were?"

"Yes." It was a whisper torn from the soul. "As I was."

Gracie sighed, smiled, shifted the baby in her arms to free one hand so she could massage Catrina's stiff shoulder. "Parents can't protect children from life, Catrina. They can only help them deal with it."

There was more truth to that than she wanted to accept. "Parents can protect children by not allowing them to stumble into dangerous and avoidable situations."

"Marriage is a dangerous situation?"

"Yes. Fortunately, it's also avoidable."

Grace considered that. "Yes, it is." A sly gleam lit her pale eyes. "But love isn't. It seeks us out when we least expect it, slams into our heart like a spiked sledgehammer, and changes us forever whether we like it or not."

The wisdom of her words sent a chill down Catrina's spine. Love was a killer of spirit in her experience, a cruel mistress that enveloped the unwary as sweetly as scented honey, a sticky prison from which escape was nearly impossible.

"Love taints our lives," she murmured. "There was a time I fantasized about love, believed in my adolescent foolishness that such profound emotion would complete us somehow, enhance our humanity. I was mistaken."

"Were you?"

"Yes." There was no quaver in her statement. The word was flat, firm. Certain. "Love is for losers, Gracie, a crutch for people too frightened to face the world on their own.''

The edge to her own voice struck deep into Catrina's heart, surprising her. There wasn't a bitterness to the words, only a resigned sadness that she hadn't recognized in herself, let alone acknowledged.

"That sounded cold," Catrina whispered. "I didn't mean it quite that way."

Actually, she had meant it exactly that way. And that frightened her.

She felt his presence even before she saw him, felt it in the warmth spreading down her spine, a gentle prickling sensation on her nape. A pleasant glow emanated from deep inside her chest, throbbing with more power as he jogged into place beside her.

"So..." He puffed a moment, and she slowed her pace for him. "Did you like the flowers?"

"What woman wouldn't like crimson roses delivered to her door in a crystal vase?" An angled glance caught the flicker of relief in his eyes, and satisfaction. "You needn't have done it, though."

"I wanted to."

"Why?"

"Because I thought—well, I hoped—that you'd enjoy them. And then perhaps you'd forgive me for my original buffoonish faux pas."

"The panty-hose incident was already forgotten."

"Forgotten?" He hiked a brow with exaggerated skepticism, which for some reason amused her.

"Perhaps not forgotten, but certainly forgiven. It isn't necessary to shower me with gifts to atone for a joke gone bad, you know."

"It's one of my greatest pleasures to shower nice people with gifts."

"So I've noticed." She slowed to a stop, stretched her tight muscles beneath an ancient, sprawling oak. For some reason she wasn't in the mood to continue her ritualistic route. She didn't feel much like running. Constant movement made it difficult to focus on the man beside her, to absorb the nuance of his expression, the lovely grin that did peculiar things to her heart.

He puzzled her. She didn't understand why she was so drawn to Rick Blaine, particularly now when the complication of a man in her life was such a harrowing thought.

"Why do you feel it necessary to buy people's affection?" she asked suddenly.

The question clearly startled him. "I don't."

"Don't you?"

He frowned. Not an angry frown, but a bewildered one that was oddly touching. "Material things may not be crucial to the overall scheme of life, but they bring solace, comfort and pleasure to those who haven't had access to them. I know what it's like to yearn for a warm jacket without holes in the elbows, a pair of shoes that hasn't already been worn by a stranger or to see a frivolous toy under a barren Christmas tree."

"So your family wasn't wealthy, I take it."

"Hardly." There was no anger in his gaze, no glimmer of self-pity. "My mom worked herself sick just trying to keep a roof over our heads. She never had anything pretty for herself, never owned a piece of jewelry that didn't turn her skin green, or an elegant dress that would make her feel like a princess, if only for a few fleeting hours. It hurt that others had so much while the woman who was the center of my universe had so little."

The loving light in his eyes as he spoke of his mother struck a familiar chord in Catrina's heart. "I know what you mean. That sounds exactly like the hardship my own mother endured when she was alive."

Rick's eyebrows furrowed into a worried line. "I'm sorry for your loss."

"It was a long time ago."

"But it's still a loss."

"Yes." A lump wedged in her throat. She whispered around it. "It's still a loss."

He shuffled in place for a moment, then flopped onto the grass beneath the shady, gnarled oak limbs. Catrina sat beside him without comment.

"You see, that's the thing," he said with an appealing hint of drawl. "Life is terminal. None of us can predict when those we love will leave us. All we know is that nothing is forever, so we share the joy of their presence while we are blessed with it, and try to minimize the regrets that will haunt us later, when it's too late to make amends."

"Do you have regrets, Rick?"

"We all have regrets, I think. If we're honest with ourselves, we'll acknowledge them." He plucked a blade of grass, rolled it between his thumb and forefinger. "Luck has smiled upon me for most of my life. I have so much more than I'll ever need. It gives me joy to share it with others, yet you see that as buying affection. Why?"

A flush of warmth rushed up her throat. "Perhaps I spoke out of turn. I meant no insult."

"None was taken. I just wondered why you gave sinister meaning to simple acts of kindness."

The conversation had veered into realms much deeper, much more personal than Catrina could have imagined. A niggling alarm whispered in her mind, a warning that she was opening her soul in a way that she'd never done before. There was something about this man that breached her defenses, lured her deepest secrets, her most private thoughts from the vault in which she'd hidden them from the world.

"Kindness is just another form of currency," Catrina heard herself say. "People use it as barter, to get what they want."

Rick studied her for a moment, then flicked the blade of grass away, turning to regard her more thoroughly. "Is that what you truly believe?"

"It's what experience has taught me." Uncomfortable now, she tucked her feet underneath her, absently smoothed the warm fleece sweatpants buckling across her thighs. "I know it sounds cynical and perhaps it is, but when you think about it, most people expect their acts of kindness to offer something in return, even if that something is esoteric or religious rather than material. For example, you've already said that bringing happiness to others makes you feel good. So an astute debater would declare that your motive for being kind is simply to feel better about yourself. It's a fine motive to be sure, but it's a motive nonetheless."

When she risked a covert glance, she saw that he was not looking at her. Instead, his gaze floated in midair, as if her words had brought forth some deeper meaning for him. "Your assessment of me is correct, I suppose. In fact, your entire argument is not only lucid and logical, but simplistically brilliant." The sliver of a smile tugged the corner of his mouth. "It's such a shame that you're wrong."

She laughed. "Why am I wrong?"

"You are wrong," he said slowly, "because I have seen the face of true sacrifice offered with no earthly or heavenly hope of reward, simply for the sake of love."

"Your mother?"

"Yes."

Catrina didn't know why she felt compelled to touch his hand. She brushed her fingers across his knuckles, cupped the back of his hand beneath her palm. It was a strong hand, so much larger than hers that the difference was startling. She hadn't noticed that about him before, hadn't noticed the strength and power of his hands. The fact that she hadn't noticed was telling, as was the fact that she made the observation now without any innate fear gnawing at her belly.

"I think," she said slowly, "that the love a mother feels for her child is the purest form of goodness that humans are capable of. In that regard, you have won the discussion."

Laugh lines crinkled the corners of his eyes. "Oh, goodie. What's my prize?"

Chuckling softly, Catrina realized that her hand was still resting on his. Withdrawing her touch, she made a production of combing fragrant blades of grass with her fingers and tried to ignore a peculiar sense of loss. "Careful now, or you'll end up proving *my* point about the inherent selfishness of human nature."

"Oh, that point was never in doubt. We are naturally narcissistic creatures, yet I still believe that such biological flaws can be overcome by the goodness of the heart."

"You are a hopeless romantic."

"Thank you." He brightened. "Speaking of which, I brought you a gift."

Catrina groaned. "Haven't I made myself clear on that topic?"

"Perfectly clear." Grinning madly, he dug under the floppy hem of his sweatshirt to a zippered pouch affixed to his waist with a nylon belt. "But I suspect you'll like this one." With a flourish, he pulled a small white bag out of the pouch, and handed it to her.

Curiosity overcame common sense. She peeked into the bag, emitted a whoosh of delight. "Coconut macaroons? I adore them! How did you know?"

"I didn't. But I adore them too, and since we are clearly soul mates—"

"Soul mates?" Her head snapped around. "Wherever did you come up with such a cockeyed notion?"

"I've always loved that term. *Soul mates*. It's so—" he dug his fingers into the bag she held and pulled out a plump macaroon "—romantic." He popped the morsel into his mouth, chewing with gusto and making "umm-umm" sounds.

Catrina saw the teasing glint in his eye and couldn't suppress a smile. Nor could she suppress her desire for one of those cookies. She ate one, closed her eyes and moaned with pleasure.

"There's a gift I hope you don't plan to return," Rick said with a smile.

She laughed. "No, and I'm not going to return this one either." She gobbled another macaroon without the slightest hesitation and languished against the tree, sated and comfortable. "It's been ages since I've had a good macaroon. Nobody in my family ever liked coconut. My sisters gag at the sight of it and Heather breaks out in a rash if she eats anything containing the merest hint of it."

"They don't know what they are missing."

"So I've told them. They are not impressed." She brushed her palms together, laid the macaroon bag aside. "There's one left."

"Want to fight for it?"

"No, you may have it."

"Aha! A selfless act of kindness." He ate the last cookie, wadded up the bag and tossed it into a nearby trash receptacle. "I knew you weren't as cold as you'd like people to believe."

The joking statement pierced her like steel. "I don't want people to believe that I'm cold."

"Don't you?" He tilted his head, regarded her with a look she couldn't quite fathom, but which heated her to the marrow. "Then why do you pretend to be tough and unfeeling when both of us know that underneath that cynical shell is a vibrant, hot-blooded woman who wants nothing more than to love and be loved?"

The question stunned her, not only the impertinence of it but the secret truth it uncovered. "My innermost thoughts and feelings are not a topic I wish to discuss."

"In that case, we won't talk. But I do plan to kiss you, kiss you as you've never been kissed before. Unless, of course, you can give me one good reason why I shouldn't."

For the life of her, Catrina could not come up with that reason. Even more distressing, she didn't want to come up with one. She wanted Rick to kiss her, wanted it more than she wanted her next breath.

And the intensity of that longing scared her to death.

Chapter Five

The words slipped from his tongue so smoothly that he hadn't realized he'd said them until he saw her eyes widen in surprise, then darken with smoldering anticipation. This was without doubt a woman waiting to be kissed, a woman *needing* to be kissed.

And for some reason Rick chose not to explore, he desperately needed to kiss her, needed to hold her, touch her, draw her essence into the starving void inside his chest.

His arms encircled her of their own volition, without conscious thought. She melted, boneless and warm, fitting her body to his with such rapturous wonder that a radiance glowed deep inside him, spreading outward like an ever-expanding star.

"You are beautiful," he heard himself whisper.

"Am I?" A breathless question, uttered into fragrant breath mingled in the tiny space between their lips.

"Yes." He caressed her cheek with the palm of one hand while the other slipped effortlessly around to the small of her back, drawing her even closer. Her hands rested against his chest, loosely curled fingers twitching ever so slightly.

She was so close, so exquisitely close, that he could see the dewy reflection of light dancing on her moist lips, feel the heat of need radiating from her skin. A delicate tremble worked through his chest. It took a moment for him to realize he was the one who was trembling.

His mouth tingled in anticipation. His heart raced, his pulse pounded. In the space of a heartbeat, he tightened his grasp, and took her lips fully, completely, in a kiss that struck like an arrow to his heart.

Colors exploded in his mind, shards of emotion he'd never experienced sliced through the very core of his soul. It was a kiss unlike any he'd ever experienced, sweet as honey, hot as a thrusting dagger, a kiss that shattered him inside and out.

A tiny moan slipped from her tongue to his and then back again. He felt her fingers curl tight against his chest, then grasp his neck to pull him closer, and closer still.

Emotion swelled inside like a tidal wave, cresting upwards until he felt as if he could no longer breathe with the force of it, and would die of its power.

Just when his spinning world seemed destined to explode, she gasped, pushed him away, and held him at arm's length. "Stop." She gulped for air, turned her face away. "Don't...please."

It took a moment for him to find his voice. "I'm

sorry. I thought you wanted me to.... I mean, I thought it was all right, that you'd..."

His foolish stutter drifted into silence. She simply shook her head, moistened her lips. "It's not your fault. I allowed myself to be swept up in the moment."

"And that was a bad thing?"

"Yes, it was." She recovered her composure considerably faster than Rick was able to recover his. "I apologize if I've led you to believe that I'm interested in playing romantic games with you. I'm not. I'm not interested in a relationship, not even a fluffy, fun one. There's simply no room in my life for another complication, and there certainly isn't any room in my life for an enjoyable romp with the playboy of the year."

Alerted by a draft on his tongue, Rick closed his mouth. He swallowed, shook his head, tried to replay her startling proclamation in his mind. "Playboy of the year? Me?"

She flushed. "I meant no insult. The truth is that I've never met anyone as well liked by so many people. You seem able to charm the fleas off a starving dog."

The last statement was tinged with enough wryness to send a chill down his spine. "A talent I've never attempted, actually, although I imagine that it could be quite useful to the pet lovers of the world."

Again she flushed, this time more with embarrassment than anger. "That wasn't meant as an insult."

"Where did you learn that it's okay to insult people if you repeatedly proclaim that said insult wasn't meant?"

A shrug, a sigh, and when she met his gaze he saw no sinister intent in her eyes. "I am brutally candid on occasion. It's a flaw, I know. However, if reality is insulting, it's not really my problem, is it? I don't need the aggravation of being another notch on your belt, Rick. I know myself. I am not emotionally able to flit from fling to fling just for the fun of it, and at this point in my life I simply do not want, nor do I need, the complication of a committed relationship."

"Committed?" He felt the blood drain from his face. "I just kissed you, that's all. No big deal." It had been a very big deal, but merely hearing the *C* word out loud had chilled his ardor more effectively than a dip in a glacial pond.

With a level gaze she said, "I know that a kiss is no big deal to you, just as I know that I am no big deal to you. What I don't understand is why you are pursuing me."

It was a question for which he was completely unprepared. "I don't know. It's not my habit to chase women who do not return my interest."

"Isn't it?"

"No." He felt his hackles rise a bit. "I happen to like people, especially women. I enjoy friendships with them. Is that a crime?"

"So that was just a 'let's be friends' kiss?"

"Of course," he lied. She was cornering him, cornering his emotions, forcing him to express motives that he didn't even understand himself. He raked his fingers through his hair, muttered to himself. "I'm sorry you find my attentions so aggravating."

Her gaze softened. She laid a gentle hand on his

arm. "Forgive me, I didn't mean to hurt your feelings."

"You didn't." Another lie. Damn. For a man who took pride in his honesty he was surprisingly skilled at prevarication. "I seem to have expressed myself badly here. I'd hoped we could be friends, that's all." And yet another bald-faced falsehood.

"I know that, Rick. Oh, I'll admit that at first I was prideful enough to believe that your interest in me was more personal, but as I've gotten to know you through the eyes of your friends I realized that you are simply a unique person with the ability to make everyone think they are special."

"This is a flaw?"

"Of course not, it's a wonderful gift." She chewed her lip, glanced away. "I want us to be friends, Rick, but on a less personal level."

He blinked in astonishment. How often had he said the same words to others? More often than he could count. And every time, the recipients of that practiced speech had gazed up with moist eyes, tremulous smiles, to agree with him. He'd thought he'd merely been honest, offering reasoning logic with which they'd sincerely agreed. After all, every woman he'd ever dated remained a dear and cherished friend. Was that a crime?

"Rick?"

"Hmm? Oh. Of course, I understand completely." It was a wonder his nose hadn't grown a foot by now.

"Great." Her smile sent an army of goose bumps marching down his spine. She glanced at her watch, immediately jumped up and brushed grass from her sweatpants. "Lordy, look at the time. I'm late." She favored him with another radiant smile. "Thanks for the cookies and for being such a terrific guy."

He offered a thin smile. "Sure, any time."

He sat as if rooted beneath the gnarled oak limbs, watching her jog fluidly down the curving park path until she disappeared from sight. Something had happened here, something frightening, something wonderful, something he did not understand and feared examining too closely.

Catrina Jordan had managed to peek into the secret recesses of his mind and his heart, and see what lurked there with more clarity than he'd believed possible. In so many ways she'd been right about him.

She'd also been very wrong. One way or another, Rick was determined to prove it. Too bad he didn't have a clue how to do that.

The brisk breeze wasn't nearly cold enough to chill her fevered skin or cool the inferno blazing deep inside. Catrina ran until sweat blinded her, ran until her lungs felt as if they would burst from the effort.

She exploded from the park, dodging pedestrians on the sidewalk and dashing into the lobby of her office building as if the devil himself was chasing her. She charged directly into an open elevator and hit the button to the health-center floor with enough force to snap her thumbnail off. Only after the elevator jerked and hummed upward did she allow herself the luxury of sagging against the mirrored walls to gasp for breath.

What had happened to her? What had happened to the tight shield she'd erected around her heart to protect her from the same surge of emotions that now threatened to choke her?

Rick Blaine had slipped past her defenses, awakened desires and longings she'd thought were safely locked away. Why had she allowed that to happen?

The elevator doors whooshed open, startling her. Still breathing hard, she stumbled to the locker room, dumped her sweats into a heap on the floor and nearly dove into the women's shower.

An icy blast of frigid water made her gasp and shiver. She relished the discomfort, focused upon it. Tears swelled behind her closed eyelids, tears of regret that she'd disguised her own emotional turmoil with unkindness. She'd seen the hurt in Rick's eyes when she'd so off-handedly called him a playboy. Deep down, she'd known the accusation was unfair, and probably untrue as well. Women were attracted to him not only because of his stunning looks, but because he had a kind heart, and truly cared about the feelings of others.

It was that unique ability to touch the hearts of others that made him so dangerous. Catrina could deal with men who were selfish, callow, who viewed others in terms of the pleasures they could offer, the needs they could fulfill. Such men had affected her life many times over the years, beginning with her father's abandonment and ending with betrayal by a man who had vowed before God to love her forever.

Yes, Catrina understood such men and had constructed an effective defense against the emotional assaults to which she had once been so vulnerable.

But she had no defense against sincerity, kindness,

a gentle spirit and a caring soul. She had no defense against Rick Blaine.

One thing she had learned about herself was that her own ability to objectively and accurately judge the motives of others was sorely flawed. She had a tendency to see what she wanted to see, not what was clearly there. There was no reason to believe she'd suddenly developed a psychological clairvoyance where Rick Blaine was concerned. Just because her heart told her that Rick was a man of honesty and principle didn't mean that it was true. Her heart had lied to her before.

She couldn't take the chance of being wrong, not again. It wasn't just her own heart she'd be risking, but her daughter's heart as well. And that was a gamble Catrina simply wasn't willing to take.

"Good morning," the receptionist said with an irksome chirp.

Rick nodded as he strode past her desk, was vaguely aware of her startled gaze following him. Only then did he realize that he'd not smiled at her, nor returned her greeting as was his custom.

He'd make amends later, after he'd learned why Catrina hadn't been at the coffeehouse this morning. Meeting her there had become a welcome part of his routine. Only when he'd spent thirty minutes milling about the crowd, straining to see her face in a sea of yawning strangers did he feel the panic rise in his chest. That's when he realized just how deeply she had burrowed into his life.

He paused outside the executive suites, rocked back on his heels, then pivoted smartly and headed back to the elevator. Two minutes later he stepped into the accounting office. He strode past the recalcitrant collator where he'd first spotted Catrina.

When he rounded the corner and saw her vacant desk, his heart nearly stopped. The computer hadn't been turned on, and the desk surface was neat, devoid of scattered papers or other evidence that it had been recently occupied.

From the corner of his eye, he saw Frank emerge from the director's office. Rick whirled on him. "Where is she?"

Frank removed his reading glasses and glanced up from the papers he'd been scanning. "Where is who?"

"Catrina." Rick knew he sounded hoarse, almost desperate. To his horror, he saw his own finger frantically waggling in the direction of her desk. "Did she call in sick?"

"Ah..." Frank followed his gesture, clearly perplexed. "No, she didn't call in—"

"She hasn't quit, has she?"

"I certainly hope not. She's an excellent accounting clerk. I'd hate to lose her."

So would Rick. "Then why hasn't somebody followed up to find out where she is and make certain she's all right?"

Frowning, Frank tucked his glasses in the breast pocket of his suit coat. "She's at the software indoctrination seminar."

"The what—?" Reason dawned slowly, along with a rush of embarrassment as he realized what a fool he'd just made of himself. "Oh. That."

A glimmer of a smile tugged the corner of the

finance director's mouth. "Yes, that pesky little training session that you insist every employee outside of the mailroom attend so they can actually figure out how this damnably complex computer system works."

"Ah. Well." He cleared his throat. The sessions were held quarterly, so Rick rarely paid much attention to the actual dates they were scheduled. He left those details up to the department managers and personnel. "I see."

"What did you need? Perhaps someone else can help you."

"Hmm? Oh, nothing important."

"Are you sure?"

"Yes, I'm sure." Rick narrowed his gaze. "Wipe that smug grin off your face."

"I'm trying."

"Try harder." Frustrated, Rick raked his hair, glanced around to assure himself that no one beyond Frank had observed his ill-timed bout of hysteria. A couple of accounting clerks glanced away much too quickly for comfort. He cringed, forced a casual tone. "By the way, where is the seminar being held this month?"

"In Tahoe." To his credit, Frank managed to keep a straight face. "Barely a two-hour flight in a rented plane."

"Thanks for the travel tip." Rick quelled him with a look. Or at least, he tried to.

Frank merely gazed back with an insufferable twinkle in his eye. "You're welcome."

"Are the budget revisions finished yet?"

"Nope."

"Well...get on it."

"Will do." Frank saluted smartly, then ambled off chuckling to himself.

Rick jammed his hands in his pockets, wandered back to the elevator and wondered if he was the last person on earth to notice that he had completely lost his mind.

Carrying his suit coat over his shoulder, Rick dragged himself up the familiar stairway, gave a perfunctory rap on the door, then opened it and walked inside. He tossed his coat over the sofa and dropped into the cushions with a sigh.

"Is that you, dear?"

He rubbed his stinging eyes. "Yes, Mom, it's me."

"I'll be right out."

"Take your time. Dinner reservations aren't for another hour."

He heard her footsteps in the kitchen, but didn't bother to open his eyes as they moved into the living area. "What dinner reservations?"

Rolling his head, he massaged his stiff neck. "I decided we needed a night out," he murmured. "Get your glad rags on, Mom, we're going to paint the town—" He glanced up, did a double take and nearly swallowed his tongue. "What is that?"

"It's a baby. You know, a small human, still in the growing stage." She shifted the gurgling toddler in her arms. "Obviously, I have plans for the evening. You should have called."

"What are you doing with a baby? Please tell me

you didn't take my 'rent a grandchild' remark to heart."

"I'm watching her for a friend." Gracie sniffed the air, frowning. "Oh, dear. The meat loaf is burning. Keep her out of mischief for a few minutes, will you?"

With that, Gracie dropped the drooling child in Rick's lap and disappeared before he could issue a protest. Stunned, he stared at the rosy-cheeked child. She giggled, jammed her pudgy fingers into her mouth, and drooled all over herself.

Rick was horrified. "Mom!"

"I'll just be a minute," came the singsong reply.

Heather giggled again, and, to his shock, wrapped her wet fingers around his silk tie. "You daddy?"

"Good heavens, no!"

Startled by his vehemence, the child widened her eyes. Her mouth quivered.

He instantly softened his tone. "I'm sorry, I didn't mean to frighten you. No, I'm not your daddy. My name is Rick. What's your name?"

The baby sniffed, regarded him warily. She was an adorable child, with huge amber eyes, a head full of blond ringlets and a tiny bow mouth that seemed vaguely familiar. "Hetter."

"Hetter?" He frowned, considered that. "You mean Heather?"

She nodded.

"That's a pretty name," he told her, and was rewarded by a tremulous smile.

"Gamma Gacie give me cookies."

"Grandma Gracie? *Grandma?*" He glanced up, astounded, as his mother emerged from the kitchen.

"When I told you to rent a grandchild, Mother, I was clearly joking."

Gracie shrugged. "Joking or not, I told you I was going to get myself a grandbaby with or without you. Now, the meat loaf is ready. Are you staying for dinner or not?"

Rick glumly eyed the wet finger marks on his expensive tie. "I'm staying."

"Good." She lifted the child from his lap, pausing to scrutinize him as only a mother could. "Go wash up, and splash your face with cold water. You look like hell."

He stood, smiling, and planted an affectionate kiss on her cheek. "You always did know how to make me feel better."

"That's what mothers are for." Shifting Heather in the crook of her arm, she freed one hand to pat his face and smooth the front of his shirt. "After dinner, you can tell me all about the latest crisis in your love life."

"What makes you think there's a crisis in my love life?"

"Just a wild guess." She gave him an amused glance. "Or perhaps it's the glassy desperation in your eyes."

"Can't a man have any secrets around here?"

"I'm your mother, not your priest. You want to keep secrets, go to confession."

"I'd love to, but we're Methodists."

"A picky point." She hurried into the kitchen and tucked the drooling baby into a high chair with practiced efficiency.

Rick had to admit his mother looked very comfortable caring for a toddler. Very comfortable and very happy.

"Now sit," Gracie commanded of him when he returned from washing up. "Sit, eat and then we'll talk about how to convince this reluctant young lady that you're not just stringing her along."

Rick's fingers froze on the back of the chair he'd just pulled out. "Stringing her along? Where on earth did that come from?"

"Mother's intuition," Gracie said, sliding into her own chair without meeting Rick's stunned gaze. "Every woman wants to believe that she is unique in the eyes of a man who interests her."

Sighing, Rick sat down without bothering to quiz his mother on her clairvoyance. He'd long ago given up trying to figure out how she knew what she knew. "How am I supposed to convince her of that? She's already made up her mind that I'm an office Lothario who woos every new employee with lecherous glee."

"Are you?"

"Of course not."

"Why do you suppose she believes you are?" The offhand question was posed as Gracie slipped a huge slab of succulent meat loaf onto his plate.

"I don't know."

"You don't?" She hiked a brow, shrugged, then proceeded to chop up a portion for little Heather, who was eyeing the preparation with obvious anxiety. "Well, if you don't know why she believes what she believes, then you're not in a position to correct her errant presumptions, are you?"

Rick glumly stared at his meal. "All I know is

that she's out of town for a few days, and suddenly I feel completely adrift, as if I don't know what to do with myself."

"You miss her."

"There's no reason why I should. I mean, I've only known her a few weeks. I haven't even dated her, unless you call huffing through the park like a pair of fleece-clad masochists to be a date. It's just that…" He sighed, forked up a hunk of meat loaf, but stopped short of actually popping it into his mouth. "I don't know how to explain it. I feel empty inside."

"You miss her," Gracie repeated, dabbing meatloaf sauce from the corner of Heather's mouth.

"Yes, I miss her."

"So why are you telling me instead of her?"

"Because you are here and she isn't."

"Do you know where she is?"

"Yes." He laid his fork down. "Do you think I should go to her?"

"What I think doesn't matter, dear. What do you think?"

"I think," he said, pushing his plate away, "that it's a lovely night to fly."

With that, he brushed a quick kiss on his mother's cheek, stroked the toddler's silky curls, and headed toward the airport.

Chapter Six

"Did you make sure she had her stuffed bunny? She can't sleep without her stuffed bunny—"

"Yes, dear." A slight chuckle filtered over the phone line. "Heather is sleeping as we speak with the crumpled ear of her beloved bunny grasped in her tiny hand."

"Oh." Catrina didn't know whether to sigh in relief, or sob with disappointment that her daughter was so apparently oblivious to her absence. She shifted the receiver, perched on the edge of a hotel mattress so hard that even the thought of sleeping on it evoked images of camping atop a boulder. "That's...good. I was concerned that she might have difficulty falling asleep, since I wasn't there to tuck her in. I always tuck her in."

A lump caught in Catrina's throat. It annoyed her. She coughed it away with a tight laugh. "Is this ridiculous, or what? I thought *my* mother was overprotective and paranoid, but I'm beginning to make her look like the queen of permissive parenthood. It's not that I have any fears about leaving Heather with you—"

"Pish, not another word." The chide was issued with a smiling voice, the hint of an imagined grandmotherly grin. "It's perfectly normal to miss your baby, to fret about her when she's out of your sight. Fretting is what mothers do best."

"Well, I'm certainly quite good at it. Expert, in fact." She fingered a padded room-service menu lying beside the telephone, glanced around the neatly appointed room, and realized that she'd never felt more alone in her entire life. "I don't suppose you'd like to bundle Heather up and drive to Tahoe for a few days, would you? They say it's going to snow tomorrow. Heather's never seen snow."

Gracie's voice softened with empathy. "The time will pass quickly once the seminar begins and you have something to focus on besides the emptiness of a sterile hotel room."

Stunned at the perception, Catrina found herself staring over her shoulder as if expecting to see Gracie's smiling image floating beside the window. "Either you are incredibly psychic, or I am incredibly transparent."

"Perhaps a bit of both?"

"Perhaps—" A sharp rap on the door jolted her. "Oh, shoot. I think the room-service guy is here to pick up the tray."

"I'll let you go, dear. Don't worry about a thing. Heather and I will be just fine."

"I know. I'll call you—" There was a muffled

click before the dial tone buzzed in her ear. "Tomorrow," she finished lamely.

She cradled the receiver with a sigh, frowned as another knock, this one louder and more insistent, jarred her to the core.

"All right, I'm coming!"

Irked by the intrusion, she marched into the tiny foyer and yanked open the door, expecting a smiling server prepared to whisk away remnants of the $25 tuna sandwich she'd picked at for supper. Instead she saw a pair of trousered legs and a string-tied mass of helium balloons.

A vaguely familiar voice echoed from behind the floating bouquet. "Delivery for Ms. Catrina Jordan."

"What on earth—?" She narrowed her gaze, parted the balloon mass and exhaled all at once. "I don't believe this."

Rick grinned. "I happened to be in the neighborhood."

"Give me a break."

"That's exactly what I intend to do." He turned sideways, herding the bouncing balloons through the doorway before Catrina could do more than flatten herself against a wall to keep from being entangled. "All work and no play makes Catrina cranky, I see."

"I am not cranky." She shut the door, folded her arms. "And since the seminar doesn't start until tomorrow morning, the only work I've done is haul luggage up an elevator and press my power suit with a travel iron."

"You carry your own luggage and iron your own clothes?" He clicked his tongue. "You really are the hands-on type. Ever heard of valet service?"

"Too expensive."

"This is a business trip. Your expenses will be reimbursed by the company."

"Oh, goodie. Then I can afford another stale tuna sandwich tomorrow night. So much excitement, my little heart might just explode."

"Not a particularly stoic traveler, I see. Ah well, not to worry." He retrieved a pearl-tipped hatpin from the inside pocket of his sports coat, and offered it to her. "Choose an adventure."

"Excuse me?"

He gestured toward the colorful array floating around his head, then held the hatpin out until she finally accepted it. "Go ahead. Pop one and see what happens."

"Hotel security will probably show up with guns drawn."

"Then I shall fling myself over your body, and protect you with my life."

She tried not to smile, she really did, but his grin was so endearing, the excited sparkle in his eyes so infectious that she found herself caught up in the spirit of play. Muted shadows inside each balloon piqued her interest, made her pulse race with childlike anticipation. "Any particular color I should go for first?"

"Since you ask—" he glanced at his watch "—yellow."

"Yellow?" To her horror, a giggle slipped from her lips. She cleared her throat, tried to maintain a modicum of dignity, only to yelp at the loud pop as she poked the yellow balloon with the pin. With a gleeful giggle she watched a pair of rectangular objects fluttering to the floor. "What are they?"

"Pick them up and see."

She grinned, scooped them up and felt her jaw droop in shock. "Tickets to David Copperfield's magic show?"

"Technically, Mr. Copperfield prefers to be called an illusionist." He feigned indifference, but the light in his eyes revealed that her joy had pleased him immensely. "It's the 10:00 p.m. show, so we only have an hour. The way you're going, it'll take that long for you to get to the next balloon."

"You mean there's something different in each of them?"

He taunted her with a grin. "Gee, I don't know. Why don't you burst them all and find out?"

This time she didn't even attempt to suppress her giggle. She stabbed a red balloon, laughed out loud as a folded receipt floated into her greedy hands. "A luncheon cruise on the *Tahoe Queen?*"

"You have to eat, don't you?" He shrugged. "The seminar breaks at 11:30, reconvenes at 2:00 p.m. I'll have you back in plenty of time for the afternoon session."

"This is better than Christmas." Wielding the pin like a sword, she advanced. "Eeny, meeny, miney—" A poke, a pop and the blue balloon expelled its prize before slumping on the end of the hanging string like a limp blue rag. "What does this mean, 'Redeemable for $50 in quarters?'"

"One cannot explore Tahoe without testing the slot machines." He frowned. "But if you don't like to gamble, you can use the money for anything you want."

Catrina remembered the whirring, flashing machines lining the hotel lobby with gaudy neon noise. "I've never played a slot machine. I don't know how."

"Ah, I shall instruct you. It's quite complex. You put the money in a slot, whereupon the machine promptly swallows your coin and either laughs in your face or spits out a thrilling quantity of new coins with a delightful chinka-chinka sound, which will intoxicate a rarely used area of the brain, causing you to feed all of your winnings back into the hungry mechanical marvel until you are utterly penniless and suicidal."

"It sounds like fun, strangely enough." She flashed him a grateful smile. "This is the nicest thing anyone has ever done for me. Thank you."

His eyes warmed. "You're more than welcome. Now burst the rest of these things. We've got places to go, and things to do."

"All right."

Breathless with excitement, she wielded her handy hatpin, squealing with delight at every magnificent prize—seasonal lift passes for a local ski lodge, dinner theater tickets for the following night and a generous gift certificate redeemable at the hotel's trendy boutique.

By the time Rick was left holding a handful of drooping strings attached to colorful latex tatters, Catrina was completely overwhelmed and nearly speechless.

"I..." She swallowed, shook her head. "I don't know what to say."

Rick eyed her anxiously. "Say you can be ready in ten minutes, so we don't miss Copperfield's opening act."

"Why are you doing this?" she blurted. The heat of embarrassment crawled up her throat. "I mean, you went to so much trouble. I don't understand. Why me?"

He studied her for a moment, then he carefully rolled up the limp strings, turning his back to her as he tossed them in the waste basket. Slipping his hands in his pockets, he rocked back on his heels, spoke without facing her. "I'm not certain I can answer that question. Why you? I don't know. Why does your image haunt me in the middle of the night? Why do I hear your laugh in my mind when I'm in the middle of a meeting or driving down the freeway? I have no idea."

He took an audible breath, shifted his stance just enough to glance over his shoulder. The sincere puzzlement in his eyes startled her and touched her deeply.

"You're special, Catrina. You affect me in ways I don't understand. I hate jogging, but I impatiently stare at the clock every morning waiting for noon so I can pant until my lungs are on fire, and torture my calf muscles into throbbing knots of agony. Why do I do that? It's insane. *I'm* insane. I can't explain it, but just being with you makes me happy." He sighed, raked his hair with his fingers. "I sound like a total idiot, don't I?"

"No." The word slid out on a sigh. "I like being with you, too."

"Do you?" He brightened, then seemed to catch himself. "I mean, you're not just saying that because I'm standing here looking pitiful, are you?"

She smiled, shook her head. "No. You do look pretty pitiful, but in an endearing and oddly appealing kind of way."

He feigned a wounded expression, although his eyes twinkled with good humor. "At least I don't have mayonnaise on my chin."

"Oh, no." Horrified, she touched a moist smear beneath her lower lip. She spun around, dashed into the tiny bathroom and groaned as she looked in the mirror. "Why didn't you tell me?"

He peered through the open door. "I just did."

"I mean why didn't you tell me earlier?" Grumbling, she snatched a towel and remedied the situation. "This is as embarrassing as posing for graduation pictures with spinach in your teeth."

"That happened to you, too? See there, we truly are soul mates."

She threw the towel at his chest.

He caught it. "I'll wait for you in the lobby. Ten minutes."

"Fifteen."

"Women," he said with a grin. "God love 'em."

Whitecaps chopped across the lake, rocking the paddle wheeler and its passengers with a rhythm that some clearly found distressing. Catrina thought it exciting. Icy air slapped her cheeks with invigorating force. A bluster of clouds wrapped dark fingers around the mountain peaks surrounding the Tahoe basin. Early spring in the Sierras was thrilling and unpredictable.

Catrina adored it. She leaned over the deck rail, squinting into the frigid spray as if to absorb every nuance of its freshness and power.

Beside her, Rick slipped a protective arm around her shoulders. "Aren't you cold?"

She nodded. "I'm freezing."

"Then let's go into the dining cabin. There's a magnificent buffet set out, and you've hardly touched it."

"I can eat and be warm any time. This could be the only chance I'll ever have to see snow fall on a mountain lake."

It amazed her that she could feel the heat of his caressing fingers through the sleeve of her thick, padded jacket. "It may not snow for hours yet. Besides, there's no law preventing you from watching through the window."

"How can I catch snowflakes on my tongue from inside the cabin?"

"Point taken." He glanced around at the few other hardy souls who'd emerged from the warmth of the dining area to brave the frigid wind. "At least we're not the only masochists on the boat...." The words dissipated slowly as Rick's gaze shifted across the deck. His brows bunched slightly, then arched with pleased surprise.

"Rick? Is that really you?"

The feminine voice echoed from behind Catrina. By the time she'd pushed back from the rail and turned to locate the source, a laughing woman was rushing into Rick's arms.

"Oh my God, how long has it been?" she gushed, hugging him fiercely.

Rick hugged her back, much to Catrina's shocked chagrin. "Too long, Janet, much too long." He brushed a kiss on her cheek, allowed her to step back even though his hands kept a proprietary grasp on her shoulders. "You are even more lovely than I recall."

That was an understatement. The woman was positively stunning, with raven hair and crystal blue eyes so exquisite that Catrina could not keep from gaping. It was rude to stare, of course, but she simply couldn't help herself. She'd never seen a woman so incredibly gorgeous in her entire life.

Her laugh was light, delicate and genuine. "You always knew the right things to say." The laugh slid into a poignant smile. "I've missed you."

"I've missed you, too."

His reply was sincere, too sincere for Catrina's taste. A pang of real jealousy startled her. It was quickly replaced by embarrassment as the woman's appraising gaze slipped gently in her direction.

Catrina absently—and foolishly—smoothed her windblown hair, as if her appearance somehow mattered to this complete stranger. For some odd reason, it mattered a great deal to Catrina. She didn't know why, but she couldn't stop herself from imagining how horrid she must look, tousled and tangled, with her lipstick chewed off and her mascara probably running from wind-induced tears.

Before she could sidestep to hide behind Rick's

substantial form, he'd expertly slipped his arm around her waist, drawing her forward. "Janet, this is Catrina Jordan."

Catrina managed a thin smile. "Pleased to meet you."

"It's nice to meet you as well."

The woman's smile was slightly sad, blatantly envious, but nonetheless sincere. Her sly gaze slipped to Catrina's left hand, as if searching for a ring, then smoothly returned to Rick with an aplomb that wouldn't have been noticeable if Catrina hadn't been studying her so intently.

"The years have treated my favorite bachelor kindly, I see." She tilted her head, gazed at him with a yearning that would have been obvious to a blind man. "Still slicing your way out of those marital nets?"

Rick didn't appear to notice that she was eyeing him hungrily. "I'm doing the female population a tremendous favor," he replied with a glib grin. "You of all people know what a rotten husband I'd make."

Catrina did a double take. *You of all people...?* Clearly these two must have shared a past considerably more intimate than Rick's platonic friendliness would imply.

To her surprise, Janet laughed at Rick's remark. "You'd make a wonderful husband. Except for that pesky commitment thing that makes you break out in a rash."

Rick laughed, too. Still holding Catrina tightly with one hand, he used the other to lift Janet's left hand, brushed the large diamond wedding band she wore with a gentle kiss. "Ah, but had it not been for my shortcomings, you wouldn't have found the man of your dreams, would you?''

A flicker of genuine pain made Janet flinch. She blinked it away, but not before the two women made eye contact. In that millisecond, Catrina realized that Janet had been deeply in love with Rick and probably still was. A gentle smile, an unspoken look, and Janet reassured Catrina that the past was behind her.

It was a strange encounter, so brief that a stopwatch couldn't have timed it; yet in that spark of a moment, the two women created a bond of understanding and empathy that was both unique and unsettling.

Rick appeared oblivious to it all. "So, where is the lucky fellow?"

Janet licked her lips and her smile quivered. She glanced away. "He, ah, had other commitments. His son from a previous marriage.... There was this camping trip, you see, and his ex-wife..." she uttered a nervous laugh, "...lovely woman, actually, but she'd forgotten to tell him about it, so we'd made plans to celebrate our anniversary here this weekend...." She licked her lips again, as if the telling gesture would detract from the bright moistening of her eyes.

The glimmer of a frown creased Rick's brow, but only for a moment.

"He'll be here in a couple of days," she said with a bit too much emphasis. "Perhaps you can meet him then."

Rick squeezed her hand. "Perhaps."

"I hope it will warm up later in the week. My husband truly hates the cold." Janet blinked, retrieved her hand and tucked it in the pocket of an expensive, fur-trimmed car coat. She made a production of staring across the lake. When she looked back at Rick, her gaze was steady. She'd regained control. "I have friends waiting for me. It really was lovely to see you again—and nice to meet you, Catrina."

Catrina accepted her handshake. She liked this woman. "It was nice to meet you too."

There was a small awkward silence, followed by the perfunctory "we must get together sometime," after which Janet squared her shoulders, jammed her hands in her pockets and disappeared into the crowded boat cabin.

Rick stared after her for a long time. His expression was thoughtful, a bit sad. It touched Catrina. "She's a lovely woman," she said.

"Yes." He sighed, smiled, brushed a kiss across Catrina's forehead. "Janet is one of the brightest and kindest people I know. She deserves to be happy."

Catrina thought it best not to point out that Rick himself might just be the cause of Janet's unhappiness. "You two must have been very close at one time."

"We were."

"Did you, ah, live together or something?"

He looked shocked. "No, of course not!"

She didn't know why she was so relieved. "I just got the impression that your relationship was rather serious, that's all."

"Serious?" His blank expression implied that he truly had no clue what that word meant. "We were very close—very dear friends."

"That's all?"

"What else is there?"

"Love."

He paled. "I don't think I have the same understanding of that word that the rest of society does. Yes, I loved Janet. I still do. I love all of my friends, and I'd walk through fire for any one of them. There's nothing magical about it, nothing romantically mystical. Love is a beautiful thing, too beautiful not to be shared with all who are of value to us."

Catrina considered that and tried to ignore the warning prickle easing down her spine. "I take it you've never been 'in love.'"

"I don't know what that means."

She regarded him. "I'm not sure I do either. *Love* is such a transitory word when you think about it. There are so many things we say we love. Ice cream and ball games, fragrant flowers and stately oak trees, the ocean at sunset, the mountains at dawn. We insist quite categorically that we love these things and use the same word to convey what we feel for our parents, our children, our spouses, our friends."

For a moment he simply stared at her. Then a slow smile worked its way along his lips, curved into the groove of laugh lines bracketing an incredibly sensual and generous mouth. "Now that was deep. I knew you weren't just another pretty face."

"You're making fun of me." She laughed, not the least bit perturbed by his comment. "I do tend to spout at the least opportune moments. Please feel free to point out my pomposity whenever it rears its ugly head."

"You weren't being pompous, you weren't spouting. The truth is that I agree with you. The word *love* is so overused and misused that I doubt anyone could truly define it."

"Perhaps that's because the definition isn't the same for any two people." She sighed, gazed across the stormy lake. "Perhaps the purest definition is the deep, profound and unconditional love of a parent for a child."

"Some parents." He glanced away. "Mothers are God's gift to the universe. Fathers are a biological afterthought."

The casual tone of his voice belied the ragged pain in his eyes, a pain blinked away so quickly she wondered if she'd imagined it. "Why do you say that?"

He angled a wary glance, as if concerned that he might have offended her. "Just my own personal experience. Did you and your father have a close relationship?"

A strand of hair whipped into her face. She wiped it away, turned her face into the wind. "We had no relationship whatsoever. He left when I was about three. The truth is that I barely remember him."

He nodded. "Mine, too. Only I was five, so I still recall the big shadow of a man appearing late at night, reeking of alcohol. My mother divorced him, then set out to find a—" he raised both hands, gesturing quote marks with his fingers "—'proper father' for me."

"And did she?"

"She remarried, if that's what you mean." He rolled his head, massaging the back of his neck as if the conversation pained him. "My stepfather was an okay fellow. He worked hard, didn't drink or carouse and never yelled at me or my mom. In fact, he rarely spoke to us at all. Seems he was more interested in a cook and housekeeper than a family. I always had the feeling that my presence irritated him."

"Did you ever establish a better relationship with your stepfather?"

"I haven't seen him since I was seven. My mother divorced him, too." His smile wasn't particularly sincere. "It seems that his presence irritated her even more than my presence irritated him."

"I'm sorry."

"Why? It's human nature, I suppose. Can you dispute that a large percentage of men, I dare say even the majority of them, are simply not cut out for parenthood, as modern society defines it?"

"Well, I'm not sure what definition you mean, but I'm afraid my own experience with fathers hasn't been a heck of a lot better than yours." A raw throb worked its way down her throat. She coughed it away, feigned a nonchalant shrug. "My sisters' father left too, before I was born. My mother always said it was the way of things. Men make babies, women care for them."

Rick nodded. "Doesn't seem fair, does it?"

"No. The thing is, I've never really believed it. I mean, I had friends with fathers to die for, men who coached their softball teams, cheered like raving idiots when their kids played a turnip in the school nutrition play, who walked the dog, fed the cat, diapered the baby and actually seemed to be happy with their family lives. So they *are* out there. I just wish that my poor mother could have found one before she worked herself into an early grave trying to raise three girls on her own." She sighed. "I don't know why I'm telling you all this. I've never said these things to anyone but my sister Laura."

He brushed a fingertip across her brow, gently smoothing a windblown strand of hair away from her face. "Like I've said, we are clearly soul mates. Scars in all the same places, realistic about what to expect from life, but not jaded by our pasts."

"Speak for yourself. I'm plenty jaded."

The comment was issued in a teasing tone, but instead of laughing with her, Rick's gaze remained serious.

"No, you're not jaded," he said softly. "You're wounded. Wounds can heal."

"Perhaps." Her heart raced at the warmth of his palm against her cheek. "In fact, I'm feeling better already."

He smiled.

Chapter Seven

"Who would have thought that a machine the size of a small microwave could eat two hundred quarters in thirty minutes without so much as a burp?"

Rick paused to scoop a small pinecone out of the snow. "In all fairness, the machine in question did offer an occasional resupply of coin, which a certain wild-eyed woman jammed back into the slot with a passionate abandon that was, by the way, incredibly sensual."

"Okay, okay, so I bought into the entire package. Flashing neon, coins chinking into the payoff tray, bells, whistles and visions of riches beyond my wildest dreams...all pretty heady stuff for a country gal." Turning her head so the breeze blew the hair out of her face, Catrina tucked her hand beneath Rick's arm. She gazed at the cedar silhouetted against a radiant moon. "I had a lovely time this evening. In fact, the past two days have been magnificent. I can't recall ever having had so much fun."

"I'm glad." Illuminated by moonlight, his smile flashed like a beacon. He bounced the small pinecone in his palm, then flipped it into the darkness. "I hope it made the seminar drudgery easier to endure."

"Actually the seminar was fascinating. That software interface is more complex than any I've worked with before. Frankly, I've been scared spitless that my technological ineptitude would land me back in the unemployment line. I simply couldn't understand how the budget and design functions meshed into billing and revenue forecasting. Fascinating stuff."

"I still don't understand it." He slowed his pace, used his free hand to caress the tips of her fingers that were curled around the crook of his arm. "Fortunately, most of the talented folk who work for me do and are kind enough to cover my posterior on a routine basis."

"You really like your employees, don't you?"

"Of course. A business is basically an extended family. Courtesy and respect go a long way toward creating a pleasant environment for all concerned." He glanced sideways at her. "Why, is there someone at the office you're having difficulty with?"

"Hmm? Oh, heavens no. Everyone has gone out of their way to be helpful and supportive. It really is a wonderful place to work, Rick."

He expelled a breath, his relief evident. "I'm glad to hear that. I want you to be happy."

"You want everyone to be happy."

"Is that wrong?"

"No. A little naive, perhaps, but it's certainly not wrong."

"Naive? Me?" His laughter was robust, genuine, but with enough of a nervous twinge to imply that she might have hit a nerve. "Nobody has ever accused me of naïveté before. An interesting observation."

Shifting, he slipped her hand from his arm, laced his fingers with hers and led her to the edge of a slender creek.

As she followed him, she studied his profile, and found it strong, angular, without a trace of softness. It seemed incongruous, out of character for a man whose eyes glowed with caring warmth and whose generous mouth was always curved in the hint of a smile.

Rick Blaine wasn't really a soft man, nor was he a hard one. He was, she realized, a man of layered complexity, the life of every party yet alone in every crowd.

In so many ways, he was the most unusual man Catrina had ever met. He was certainly the most generous, the kindest, the most sincere. Every friend he made was a friend for life.

On the surface Rick Blaine was every woman's dream, the embodiment of that handsome, loving, fairytale prince that lonely little girls dream about. But just below that polished exterior lurked the shadow of a wounded warrior, a man tormented by life but never defeated by it. He was complicated, profound, a man of secret fears. He was also a man Catrina could fall in love with.

Perhaps she already had.

The niggling thought raised her pulse rate, and frightened her half to death. Love was a fool's game. It had given her nothing but grief, given her mother nothing but grief. She'd made herself a solemn promise that she'd never again allow her heart to rule her head.

Then she'd met Rick Blaine, a man who had single-handedly destroyed her belief that the male gender was incapable of selfless concern and gentle kindness.

Rick's mellow voice startled her from her reverie. "I've always been fond of this little stream," he said. "The rocks lining it are covered with rich moss and lichens in the most extraordinarily verdant hues." He slipped an arm around her shoulders, drew her in close. "It's too dark to see how clear the water is, or to appreciate the variety of water plants and ferns thriving on its banks. Nighttime doesn't do it justice. We'll have to come back in the morning."

A twinge of real regret startled her. "I can't. I have an early flight."

"Flights can be changed." Turning to face her, he kept one arm clamped around her waist, and lifted her chin with his free hand. "And if you're really feeling adventurous, you can allow me the privilege of being your personal pilot for the trip home."

"You flew yourself up here?"

"Yes, and my arms are sure tired."

Even in the dim moonlight she saw the teasing glint in his eyes. "That joke is positively ancient."

"I know, but you're supposed to laugh anyway. It's good for my ego." Dipping his head, he brushed his lips along her forehead, a casual intimacy that thrilled her to her toes. "Think about it," he whispered, his breath warm against her skin. "After you've slept in as long as you want, I'll buy you strawberry waffles with sweet cream and honey." He paused to kiss her eyebrow, her temple, the sensitive flesh beneath her ear. "Then we can spend the entire morning together, or the entire day, and as soon as you're ready, we'll gas up the plane and soar into the clouds. Just you..." he nuzzled the side of her neck "...and me..." his teeth grazed her earlobe, nearly driving her wild "...and God as our co-pilot."

She shivered as he traced the contours of her throat with his lips. "It sounds—" a tiny gasp escaped as he gently nibbled the side of her jaw "—lovely." The final word rushed out on a broken sigh.

"There's so much I want to show you." His lips were everywhere, heating her skin until it burned like glowing embers. Her pulse pounded with percussive intensity. "So much I want to share with you."

"I...really shouldn't."

If Catrina could think straight, she might have realized that staying longer was out of the question. If her heart wasn't beating like a crazy drum, if her mind wasn't spinning, if her blood wasn't rushing wildly with each touch of his lips to her burning skin, Catrina might have even remembered that she'd promised to pick Heather up by midmorning so Gracie could have the afternoon to herself.

But Catrina was not thinking straight. She wasn't thinking at all. She was awash in sensation, trembling with yearnings she'd believed long dead, but which now flared to life with such power that it would have been easier to leap off the moon than to relinquish a single precious moment with this very special man.

From what seemed a great distance, she heard a voice very much like her own. "Just let me make a quick call."

His smile was as tangible as a touch. "As luck would have it, I happen to have a phone in my pocket." He dug it out, handed it over.

She shook her head, laughed softly. "Talk about being prepared for every eventuality."

"Hey, I was a Boy Scout, you know, and a darned good one. Except for the stick-rubbing and flint-fire trick. Never got the hang of that." His lopsided grin made her laugh out loud. "I did, however, get quite clever at concealing a lighter up my sleeve."

She flipped open the phone, entered Gracie's phone number. "A cheating Boy Scout? Isn't that rather paradoxical?"

He looked stung. "I didn't cheat, I used creative innovation to achieve a positive outcome."

"So that's what they're calling it nowadays." The phone rang several times. Catrina frowned, glanced at her watch when the answering machine picked up. "That's odd," she murmured. "She certainly should be home."

Rick glanced over. "Who are you calling?"

"My babysitter." The answering machine beeped, so Catrina began her message. "Hi, it's me. Judging by the time, you're probably giving the baby a bath, so when you've wiped the bubbles out of your eyes, can you give me a call back at...wait a minute, I don't know what this cell phone number is."

She turned to Rick, only to have the question die

on her lips. Even in the dim moonlight she could see that he'd paled several shades.

"Your...babysitter?" The horror in his eyes was shattering. "You have a child?"

Catrina's heart twisted and sank. She'd seen that expression before, in her ex-husband's face the day she'd informed him that she was pregnant.

It took a moment before she could catch her breath. "Never mind," she whispered into the phone, imagining how shaky her voice would sound when Grace replayed the message. "I'll call back later."

"A child," Rick murmured to himself. He raked his hair, looked as if he might faint. "I didn't know."

She thumbed off the cell phone, handed it back and tried to shore up her emotions. "It's not a secret. I presumed that you'd seen my personnel file. My daughter is listed as my beneficiary, and of course I carry medical insurance on her."

The suggestion seemed to startle him. "I haven't looked at your personnel file. That would have been an invasion of your privacy."

"I see." She swallowed a lump, managed to speak with a coolness that didn't reveal her inner turmoil. "May I presume that children are a problem for you?"

"Ah, no, of course not. I mean, not really." That was a bald-faced lie, and Catrina knew it. Shooting her a glance, Rick clearly realized that she knew it. He sighed. "I really haven't spent much time around children, actually. Yes, I'll admit, I've avoided them. It's the father-figure thing. It terrifies me. They look up at me with such huge, hopeful eyes, as if I'm going to sweep into their lives and become some heroic savior of their young existence.... It scares me."

Catrina peeled her lips from her teeth. "I wish I'd known that."

"I would have told you if I'd realized you had a child. You've never mentioned her."

"Of course I have. I talk about Heather all the time."

"I thought you were talking about one of your sisters." His eyes widened. "Heather? Oh, God. Describe her to me."

"What? Why?"

"Tell me she isn't about two years old, with big brown eyes, curly blond hair, and a single dimple in one of her rosy little cheeks."

Catrina felt her jaw drop. "Did you see the picture I carry in my wallet?"

Rick groaned, sagged against the trunk of a nearby cedar. "No, I met the young lady in question up close and personal."

A prickle of pure dread shimmied down Catrina's spine. She licked her lips. "You're scaring me."

He shook his head, pinched the bridge of his nose. "Let's just say that your favorite babysitter and I have more than a passing acquaintance."

"How do you know Gracie?"

He sucked a deep breath. "Prepare for a shock, Catrina. You are not going to like this."

As it turned out, that chilling assumption could not have been more correct.

Three hours later Gracie opened her door with a smile, seeming not the least nonplussed by the two scowling faces that greeted her. "Well, what a wonderful surprise. Two of my very favorite people at the same time."

"Can it, Mom. We're on to your scheme." Rick's arms were folded and tucked tighter than a hotel bedsheet. "Of all the annoying, interfering games of matchmaking you've trumped up in the past, this one is without doubt the most devious."

Gracie stepped aside to allow them access, her smile not wavering in the slightest. "Why, whatever do you mean, dear? I don't recall ever having suggested you and Catrina even meet, let alone—" her grin widened in spite of an obvious effort at control "—trump up a relationship. I'm really quite mystified."

"Oh, please, don't play innocent." Rick emitted a snort. "Remember the soprano who spoke in sign language so she wouldn't damage her throat?"

Gracie chuckled under her breath. "You enjoy opera, and you detest people who talk too much. I thought you two would have a lot in common."

"The spider-woman who'd been widowed three times under dubious and suspicious circumstance?"

"Mere coincidence. Clearly she and her three beautiful children deserved a man with a stronger constitution."

"Not to mention more lucrative life insurance."

Gracie looked stung. "I certainly didn't raise you to be so suspicious."

"And there was the pregnant gymnast with seven brothers, all of whom were determined to marry her off to the first available man who stumbled into the snare. And the high-powered investment banker who wanted me to recite portfolio percentages during the more intimate moments of our relationship, the aeronautical engineer with toddler twins who quizzed me on diaper-changing techniques on our first date, the—"

Gracie held up a palm, silencing him. "They were all perfectly lovely young women, dear. You can't blame a mother for trying, can you?"

His chin drooped in a way that might have been comical under other circumstance. "I most certainly can, and I do. You promised you'd stop after that blond pyromaniac tried to set my trousers on fire."

"I did stop, dear. Just because you are attracted to a lovely young woman at the office, a young woman who coincidentally happens to be a friend of mine, well, destined serendipity is certainly beyond a mere mortal's control."

Catrina watched the interaction between mother and son, wondering why she hadn't noticed the resemblance between them earlier. Rick clearly had his mother's patrician nose, her incredibly bright blue eyes, the same tousle of unmanageably thick hair even though Gracie's was mostly gray and Rick's was still a lustrous shade of coffee brown.

Despite Rick's obvious exasperation and Gracie's feigned innocence, the affection between them was unmistakable. Under ordinary circumstances, Catrina would have enjoyed their rapid-fire banter and witty repartee.

At the moment, however, she was too wounded inside to appreciate what would have otherwise been an extremely amusing exchange between two people who clearly adored each other.

"I thought we were friends, Gracie." The whisper emanated from Catrina herself, although she hadn't planned to utter the thought aloud.

When she spoke, both Rick and Gracie fell silent, turning their gazes as if just reminded of Catrina's presence.

The sparkle of triumph immediately drained from Gracie's eyes. "We *are* friends, dear. You must know by now that I think the world of you."

"Friends don't set each other up." Catrina bit her lip, twisted her fingers together. "When you sent me to apply for that job, you deliberately avoided telling me that your son owned the company."

"Did Rick hire you?"

"Well, no, but—"

"Of course he didn't. He's clueless about personnel matters, which is why you wouldn't have gotten the job unless you'd proven yourself the best qualified to those who are knowledgeable enough to judge such things. So why should I have mentioned that my son happens to work in the same building?"

Catrina felt her skin heat. "I talked to you about him, told you about our relationship. You just sat there, grinning inside, and never let me know...." The words trailed off. She glanced away, couldn't meet Rick's horrified gaze.

He made a choking sound. "You talked to my mother about... us?"

"I didn't *know* she was your mother."

Gracie blinked. "Never fear, Rick, Catrina didn't breathe a word about the juicy personal stuff. Of course, you didn't either. Except for that time you mentioned a particular appeal to certain parts of her anatomy, and that there ought to be a law against someone looking that good in fleece joggers—''

Catrina gasped. "You said that to your *mother?*"

"Dear God, kill me now." Rick groaned, rubbing his eyes with the heels of his hands. "Is nothing sacred?"

"Ha." Embarrassed and flustered, Catrina marched across the living room and began to toss strewn baby items into the diaper bag. "This is insane. But hey, why not?" She shoved a pacifier into the bag, followed by a half-empty juice bottle. "I seem to be an insanity magnet. The good news—" she shouldered the bulging bag "—is that it serves as a well-timed reminder about the folly of emotional entanglements. For that much, I'm grateful."

"Folly?" Rick couldn't believe that anguished squeak had actually fallen from his own lips. "I don't think our relationship could be described as folly."

Across the room Catrina straightened, her eyes flashing like amber fire. She had never looked so beautiful to him. "What would you call it? A few hours ago, you considered us soul mates. Now you're all puffed up with indignation because we've both been pawns in a matchmaking manipulation so cleverly crafted that even in hindsight we can't figure out how she actually did it."

He couldn't deny that. "This is between me and a certain interfering, grandma wannabe. It has nothing to do with you."

"That is exactly my point." The fire drained from her eyes, and her shoulders slumped just enough to signal defeat. "Heather and I were just a couple of handy chess pieces for the gamesmanship between the two of you."

Her wounded expression cut Rick to the core. Before he could summon the words to dispute the indisputable, she'd pivoted on her heel and disappeared into the bedroom.

An icy void opened inside him with her absence. He didn't dwell on the sensation, turning instead to glower at the woman whose eyes no longer sparkled in triumph. "See what you've done?"

Sadly Gracie looked up, shook her head. "I've done nothing, Rick, except point a qualified accounting clerk in the direction of a job, then keep my mouth shut. You were the one who saw her across a crowded office, and fell head over heels because she was the one woman in your life who didn't fawn all over you."

He stiffened as if he'd been struck. "That's a low blow."

"But a true one nonetheless." She sighed. "I honestly believe that you were initially attracted to Catrina because of the challenge she presented. Perhaps that's all it ever was, in which case you can rest assured that your record remains unblemished. You've won. I can see from the look in her eyes that she cares deeply for you. She wouldn't be so hurt otherwise."

Before he could respond, Catrina emerged from the bedroom carrying a sleepy toddler wrapped in a blanket. The baby fussed fitfully, popped a thumb in her tiny mouth and burrowed against her mother's shoulder. Catrina smoothed the child's damp hair, whispered softly to calm her.

It was, Rick thought, one of the most beautiful and poignant sights he'd ever witnessed. Something vibrated deep inside him, something warm and wonderful and utterly terrifying. He envisioned himself standing beside them, his arm around Catrina's shoulders while he gazed at the beautiful toddler with a proud, fatherly smile on his face.

It was enough to make a confirmed bachelor weep.

Catrina shifted her precious bundle, gazed across the room with wide and wary eyes. "Thank you for watching her, Gracie. I truly do appreciate it."

"You're more than welcome, dear."

"I want to thank you, too," she told Rick without a trace of sarcasm. "I truly did have a lovely time in Tahoe. You were most...generous."

He stepped forward, extending a hand. "Catrina, wait—"

"No, really, I must get Heather home. She's exhausted, and she feels a little warm to me."

"At least let me drive you."

"Thanks, but my car is downstairs in the parking garage." As she brushed past him, the scent of baby powder mingled with the fragrance of sweet cedar and Catrina's own sensual perfume.

The effect it had on him was startling, to say the least. It took him a moment to realize that she was struggling to free a hand for the doorknob.

He sprang forward, opened the door for her. "I'll call you later. We'll...talk."

She looked up then, her eyes filled with disappointment, and with a wisdom beyond her years. "Trust me when I say that we have nothing to talk about."

Stunned, Rick stood in the open doorway until long after Catrina had stepped into the elevator and disappeared from view. "I think," he said slowly, "that she just dumped me."

Gracie walked up beside him. She patted his shoulder, clucked her tongue. "It's about time someone did."

He stared at her. "Thank you for the motherly support."

"You're welcome, dear. Would you like some tea with that comfort?"

He closed the door, leaned against the jamb. "Am I really so shallow?"

Gracie's eyes warmed. "No, you're not shallow. You're protective of your heart, and you've got your reasons. Catrina has her reasons as well. The truth is that I would never have deliberately set you up with her, because she's had one heck of a tough life, and she deserves a man who is willing to share her life, not just pass through it."

"What makes you think I'm just passing through?"

She patted his cheek, smoothed the front of his shirt. "You're my son and I love you, but we both know that you won't even buy a goldfish because it's too big a commitment."

"Maybe I'm just looking for the right goldfish."

"Maybe." The gleam in her eye announced that once again he'd slipped smoothly into her trap. "And maybe you'll take so long to decide that the right one will be swimming in someone else's aquarium before you realize what you've lost.''

The image that evoked sent a chill down his spine. "You think you're pretty smart, don't you?"

Gracie smiled. "I raised you, didn't I?"

Chapter Eight

Heather's cranky cry grated on Catrina's last nerve. "Shh, I know you're hungry, sweetie. Just let Mommy heat up the spaghetti—" The sneeze sneaked up on Catrina, spinning her around. She sneezed twice more before stumbling to the bathroom for a tissue.

Heather toddled after her. "Want cookie," she sobbed. "Firsty, Mommy, want juice."

Catrina sagged over the sink, feeling like an overcooked noodle. Her skin was on fire, and her stomach felt as if it was bouncing along an internal treadmill. "You can have a cookie after dinner."

"Want cookie now!" To punctuate the request, Heather flung herself to the floor and howled.

Groaning, Catrina held her head between her palms as if the futile effort could keep her throbbing skull from exploding. She stepped over the screeching toddler, staggered into the kitchen and was relieved to see steam rising from the small pot. She whispered a prayer of thanks for the convenience of canned spaghetti, but before she could spoon it onto her child's plate, the doorbell rang.

At least, she thought it was the doorbell. Between the watery roar in her plugged ears and Heather's shrieking tantrum, the faint jingle could have been anything from the telephone next door to the ice-cream truck tooling down the road in front of her apartment.

Scooping up her angry child, Catrina hurried across the living room mumbling motherly words of comfort that were completely ignored by the wailing, red-faced toddler. Somehow she managed to fumble the door open and found herself staring into a pair of wary, sky-blue eyes.

Rick stood there coatless, tie slightly askew, his hands stuffed in his trouser pockets. "Hi."

She managed to return the greeting before a fit of coughing turned her away. When she'd caught her breath, she realized that he'd stepped into the living room and closed the door behind him.

It had been nearly ten days since they'd returned from that fateful Tahoe trip. Rick had left the following day for New Orleans, where he'd managed to garner a lucrative design contract that was the buzz of the office. "I didn't think you were due back until later this week."

"The deal was done. There wasn't any reason to stay."

She nodded, avoided his gaze. She knew she looked like death on a stick, but was too exhausted to care. "Congratulations, by the way. You copped quite a coup. Frank was absolutely beside himself with joy. He seems to think the profits from this venture will allow a major expansion within the next five years."

Rick offered no response beyond a furtive glance at Heather. The baby had thankfully ceased screaming long enough to size up this interesting visitor with huge, tear-stained eyes. She shuddered with a remnant sob, popped a thumb in her mouth.

Rick moistened his lips, turned his attention to Catrina. "I know it's perverse," he said quietly, "but I was actually relieved to find out you'd called in sick today."

"You're right." Her own voice thrummed through the roaring in her ears, sounded like she was talking with a clothespin on her nose. "That is perverse."

"When you weren't at the coffee shop this morning, I was afraid you were just avoiding me." He tried for a smile that didn't quite come off. "So I was pleased to discover that you were merely on your deathbed."

Catrina avoided looking at him. She'd already memorized every nuance of his face, every subtle line of form and feature was etched in dreams that continued to haunt her. If she gave in, if she allowed herself to be mesmerized again by his polished prose, by the same smooth proficiency that had so recently garnered what had been considered an impossible contractual feat and which turned even devoted foes into fanatical followers, she knew that she'd be lost forever.

This was a man who had burrowed into her heart

and who would eventually have no choice but to break it.

"My mother says you haven't been around lately." Rick paused, seemed to be struggling for words. Odd for a man whose silver tongue was theoretically one of his greatest assets. "She means well, you know."

"Yes, I know." Catrina shifted her grasp as Heather spun in her arms to study the man hovering beside a sofa cluttered with baby toys. "I'm not angry with her."

"You're angry with me, though."

Catrina considered that. "No, actually I'm not. The truth is that I don't have time for you, Rick. I have a child to raise, a child that is my first, my only priority. I don't have time for anyone who doesn't understand that priority, and doesn't share it."

"I do understand." His voice was ragged, shockingly so. "Look, I'll be the first to admit I don't have much experience with children...." The speech dissipated as she hiked a brow. He sighed, allowed the hand he'd extended to drop limply to his side. "All right, I don't have any experience with children, and that has always been a conscious choice on my part."

She shrugged. "That seems to be the conscious choice of all too many men. Which pretty much proves my point." Suddenly weary to the bone, she struggled across the small kitchen to stir the steaming spaghetti and turn off the flame. "Fortunately you made that choice before producing offspring rather than after the fact. At least, one hopes so."

A glance confirmed his pained expression. "I have

not ventured forth and been fruitful, if that's what you're asking."

"I wasn't asking anything." The wooden spoon seemed to weigh a ton. She laid the drippy thing down, unconcerned by the red sauce staining her usually spotless counter. "Your personal life is none of my business."

"I want it to be your business."

"Well, I don't."

"That's becoming clear."

"Good." God, she felt hot. The room was spinning, and she felt as if she was holding an anvil in her arms instead of a small child. "Let's discuss this another time, okay? Heather is starving, and I really don't..." She swayed, swallowed a surge of nausea. "Uh-oh."

"Catrina?"

Without considering the consequence, she thrust the baby in Rick's direction, heard his grunt of surprise as she darted into the bathroom and was violently ill.

Except for the horrifying moment when Gracie had momentarily plopped Heather onto his lap, Rick had never held a child in his life. Not once. Ever.

The first thing that struck him was how light the baby felt in his arms, and how soft. Heather wrapped a pudgy arm around his neck, regarding him with sage little eyes that seemed to understand how awkward the situation was for him.

She yanked her thumb out of her mouth with a slushy, popping sound. "Want cookie," she announced.

"Er, well..." He cast a frantic eye toward the closed bathroom door. "I think your mother would prefer you have your dinner first."

Brown baby eyes narrowed, the drooling mouth puckered, and a fresh sheen of moisture leaked onto her rashy red cheeks.

Rick couldn't have been more frightened if the child had pulled a live grenade out of her diaper. "Oh God, you're not going to cry, are you? Please don't cry."

Heather shuddered, her tiny lips contorted.

Rick thought he might faint from the panic. "Wait, look, food is right here, real food—" He grabbed the spoon he'd seen Catrina using, and jammed it into a pot full of disgusting red sauce with a few pasta strings floating through it. "Um, well, maybe not real food, but the canned equivalent thereof."

To his shock, the baby flung both arms toward the pan and began to grunt wildly.

Something in his chest melted. "You really are hungry, aren't you? I guess I'd cry too if some strange fellow showed up to delay my dinner."

He spun around as Catrina emerged from the bathroom, looking pale and weak. "Are you all right?"

She nodded, sagged against the doorjamb.

Rick dropped the spoon, hugged the toddler against his chest as if she were a fat football, and hurried over to lay the back of his hand against Catrina's forehead. "You're burning up. You need a doctor."

"It's just a virus. Heather had it last week, and the doctor said it was nothing to worry about. Now it's my turn." She took a wheezing breath, wiped her face with her hands. "Obviously this isn't the best time for me to entertain unexpected guests."

"I wish you didn't consider me a guest."

She shot him a weary look. "Well, you don't look much like the maid."

"Perhaps if I wore a gingham apron?"

"Gingham would clash with your designer tie." She pushed away from the doorjamb. "I don't mean to be rude, but please go away."

"You're sick. You need help."

"Your astute observations are duly noted, and would be appreciated if you were either a doctor or a nanny. As it is, you are merely a brave-but-terrified bachelor with drool on his collar."

She was correct on all counts. Rick was totally out of his element, and he knew it. By all rights he should run, not walk, out of the apartment and out of Catrina's life, a life that was foreign to him.

"Just give me a chance," he heard himself saying. "Then if you want me out of your life, say the word and I'm gone."

Something flickered through her eyes, a flash of hope or of despair, or perhaps a combination of both. In an instant it was gone, replaced by the dull resignation of a woman all too familiar with putting her own needs aside to satisfy the whim of others.

"Okay, fine," she murmured with a glimmer of sweet retribution that Rick didn't recognize until it was too late. "Be sure to cut up the spaghetti into spoon-sized pieces, no dessert until she's finished dinner, and she prefers the pink bubble bath to the blue bath salts."

"Bath?" Rick nearly choked on the word. The

thought of grasping a splashing, slippery toddler nearly gave him a heart attack on the spot. "Actually, I was thinking more along the lines of taking care of—"

The word *you* teetered on the tip of his tongue before he reeled it back, and swallowed it whole.

"—anything you want me to take care of," he said weakly.

With a grunt and a nod, she tottered into the bedroom and shut the door.

Sighing, Catrina sat on the edge of the mattress, vaguely aware that she'd neglected to make her bed this morning. The covers were still deliciously mussed, enticingly tousled. She was tired, weary to the bone. Every joint in her body ached as if it had been hammered with a sledge. She yearned to stretch out, pull the blanket over her head, and sleep until she'd aged five years.

That's what she longed to do, but she planned only to give Rick five minutes of sheer, unadulterated panic before she reappeared and rescued him from the grip of his own misplaced kindness.

She had no doubt that his desire to help was genuine. Rick was the type of person who wanted desperately to right every wrong, bring happiness to all who crossed his path. He didn't understand that children were not a passing fancy to be placated with gifts and giggles then abandoned for the next needy cause. Children were forever, a lifetime commitment that men like Rick Blaine couldn't comprehend or appreciate.

Catrina yawned, sneezed, reached for a tissue and

glanced at the clock radio on her night stand. Just a couple more minutes, she decided. By then, Rick would no doubt have spaghetti in his hair, panic in his heart, and leave skid marks on the front stoop.

Until then, she might as well be comfortable. Leaning back, she cradled her head in the softness of a downy pillow, and promptly fell asleep.

It was the embodiment of his worst nightmare, his deepest fear. A small child, a miniature human with whom he could not hope to communicate in his normal glib and effective fashion, who was staring in hopeful anticipation of him somehow managing to meet her considerable needs.

Rick did not have a single clue how to do that.

Well, perhaps he had one small clue. He sucked a breath, muttered aloud to encourage himself. "Food. Food is easy. Plop it on a plate, watch it disappear. I can do that."

Still balancing the baby in the crook of his arm, he hustled around the cluttered kitchen, opening cupboards until he located a stash of dinnerware. He grabbed the first plate he saw, and dumped the entire contents of the pan onto it without stopping to consider the consequence. The soupy sauce overflowed the porcelain lip, and oozed onto the table. Cursing his own stupidity, Rick grabbed a handful of paper towels.

By the time he'd mopped up the majority of the mess, Heather was grunting wildly, and squirming in his arms. He gingerly sat her in a chair, then stood back, pleased with himself.

It took a moment to realize that only the child's

eyes were visible above the edge of the table. A quick glance around the room revealed a high chair, the purpose of which he cleverly, if belatedly, deduced.

Undaunted, Heather had already scrambled to her knees and gouged a handful of spaghetti from the sloppy mess on her plate. She stuffed it into her mouth, chewing happily and seemingly oblivious to the red sauce running down her chin.

Rick moaned. It was a bit late for the high chair, but clearly, some kind of utensil would be helpful in this situation. He rummaged through the drawers until he located a nest of spoons, and rushed to the table with his prize. "Here. Spoon. Eat." He displayed the item, then performed an elaborate pantomime of scooping and chewing motions.

Heather regarded him with something akin to pity, then grabbed another handful of food and jammed it into her sticky mouth.

"No, no." He stepped forward, delicately held her wrist between his thumb and forefinger, and inserted the spoon handle in her sauce-covered hand. "There. Isn't that better?"

Heather eyed him, eyed the spoon, placed a fistful of spaghetti onto the utensil and shoveled the entire gooey mess into her mouth.

This was not going well, not going well at all.

Fearing Catrina would emerge at any moment to see her child wearing her dinner rather than consuming it, Rick hesitantly attempted to remedy the situation. Holding the toddler's fragile wrist, he attempted to guide the spoon's movements. "First you scoop like this, then you—"

"No!" Heather yanked her hand from his grasp, flinging the contents of the spoon into the air. What didn't land on her own head splatted onto the front of Rick's shirt. The toddler glowered up at him.

She had spaghetti in her hair, and her scalp dripped with orange sauce. "*Me* do it."

"Yes," he said with a pained sigh. "You certainly did."

Her little brows puckered. "Firsty. Want juice."

"Juice?" He glanced around. "What kind of juice?"

Heather blinked. "Firsty," she insisted. Her lips started to quiver.

"Okay, okay, I understand. Don't cry. Dear God, please don't cry." Frantic, he found a small glass, rooted through the refrigerator until a bottle of apple juice caught his eye. "Look, juice, I'm pouring juice right now...in a glass...for you." He kicked the fridge door shut with his foot, dashed across the kitchen and set the glass down with a flourish. "There. Juice."

The child sniffed, grabbed the glass and drained it without so much as a thank-you-kindly.

Oddly enough, Rick was deflated by that. Babies, he was learning, weren't particularly adept at expressing appreciation.

They were also rather messy creatures, more so than he could have possibly imagined. By the time Heather had switched from consumption mode to play mode by finger painting the table with leftover sauce, the bath idea was looking more like a necessity than an afterthought.

It was still, however, an incredibly frightening prospect. He decided it was time to call in an expert.

"What do you mean you won't do it?" Rick stared at the telephone as if visualizing his mother's laughing face on the other end of the line. He swallowed, cleared his throat, tried for a more rational line of reason. "Perhaps I neglected to make the situation clear enough. You have to do it. A child's life is at stake."

Grace's chuckle raised the hairs on his nape. "Still overly dramatic when you don't get your way, I see."

"You don't understand—" He yelped as Heather toddled into the living room clutching a white throw pillow now decorated with orange smears. "No, no, you mustn't touch anything. Your mommy will be most unhappy with both of us."

He stuffed the ruined pillow under a sofa cushion, scooped the giggling toddler under one arm, and returned to delivering the most impassioned speech of his life to the one person who was least likely to be moved by it. "Look, I'm desperate. Please, just come over and give the child a bath before she glues herself to the carpet."

A popping sound filtered over the line, along with the snap of what sounded like a small appliance door being opened. "Hmm? I'm sorry, I missed part of that. The popcorn is ready."

"Popcorn?" Rick shifted his grasp as Heather wriggled under his arm. "*Popcorn?* I'm groveling to maintain a modicum of sanity, and you're making popcorn?"

"It's Sean Connery night, dear. I've rented two of his very best movies and am settling in for a magnificent double feature, not to mention a bit of older woman-older man sexual fantasy."

"Mother, please. I do not want to hear about your fantasies."

"Fair enough," she replied cheerfully. "By the way, dear, it was very nice of you to offer to help Catrina out. I'm sure she'll be most appreciative."

"Appreciative? The place resembles a frat house after a food fight, and the baby looks like Medusa with orange worms sprouting from her scalp." Rick groaned at his mother's amused chuckle. "Look, feeding is one thing. Bathing is something else. I've never even bathed a dog, for heaven sake."

"It's easy. Put baby in tub, lather washcloth with soap and scrub vigorously. Rinse, dry and diaper. Nothing to it."

"Diaper?" His eyes widened to the point of pain. "Good Lord, it never occurred to me that she might not be...housebroken."

"She still requires a bit of protection overnight. During the day she does fairly well at making her personal needs known." There was a clunk, followed by a peculiar noise that sounded suspiciously like popcorn being poured into a bowl. "As organized as Catrina is, I'm sure you'll find everything you need. Just open your eyes and look around."

Rick did so and saw a smeared pool of coagulated sauce and spilled juice on the kitchen floor, along with tiny footprints of the same sickly hue tracked across the living room carpet. "Please, I'm begging you. I'll pay you a hundred million dollars if you'll come over here and get me out of this mess."

"Sorry, dear. A hundred million isn't enough. I've already told you, it's—"

"Sean Connery night," he snapped. "I know."

He hung up the phone, rubbed his aching head, and groaned aloud. Skydiving without a chute would be preferable to what awaited him. He'd probably draw the water too hot or too cold, so the baby would end up with either first-degree burns or double pneumonia. Presuming, of course, he managed to keep from drowning her in the first place.

"Owie?"

"Hmm?" He glanced down, realized the poor baby was tucked under his arm like a football. He shifted her upright, held her against his shoulder with considerably more expertise than he'd done even an hour ago. "Owie? Oh, you're asking if I have a headache?"

Grinning, the baby hooked a finger over her lower teeth, and bobbed her head. She shifted, puckered her little mouth and planted a moist, saucy kiss on his chin. "There," she crowed. "All better."

Something cracked deep inside his chest. "Yes," he heard himself whisper. "It's definitely all better. Thank you."

Heather giggled, wrapped her arms around his neck. The trusting gesture did strange things to his heart.

Most children, Rick had noted, were not particularly attractive to anyone except their doting parents. Such offspring usually had grimy faces, runny noses, or were an unnatural shade of purple from their latest tantrum.

This particular child, however, was special. Yes, her face was grimy to the point of disgusting, and her hair was matted with spaghetti sauce. Yes, her little nose was even a tad runny. Of course her skin was orange at the moment rather than purple, but she was still a sweet child, even an appealing one.

Perhaps it was because she looked so very much like her mother.

He gazed into the wide, baby eyes. "You realize, of course, that I have never bathed a child in my life." Heather's eyes widened even further. "I will attempt this on the one condition. You must promise me that you will not drown."

Heather blinked, issued a somber nod.

"Very well." He stiffened his spine, sucked in a breath, and carried his grimy but precious cargo into the bathroom.

Catrina awoke with a gasp, partly because her head felt as if it might explode at any moment and partly because her nightstand clock insisted that it was nearly midnight.

Midnight.

She'd been asleep for almost five hours. Stumbling out of bed, she tripped over her own feet, lurched across the bedroom in total panic. Rick would probably be ready to kill her. Presuming, of course, he hadn't called Child Protective Services and walked out hours ago.

Not knowing what to expect, she stumbled into

Heather's room and instantly panicked. The crib was empty.

Terrified, she rushed into the kitchen, squinting at the blast of light, vaguely aware that the room seemed considerably cleaner than it had been when she'd left it. The pot in which the spaghetti had heated had been washed and stacked neatly in the drainer along with the rest of the dishes that she'd left piled in the kitchen sink.

Also, the floor had been swept and mopped. There were patches on the wall in which the paint was slightly lighter and brighter than the surrounding area, as if someone had done hasty spot cleaning. And where the living-room carpet met the kitchen tile there were several damp, footprint-sized spots that also implied an attempt at stain removal.

She emerged into the living area, saw that the television was on. An old western movie was playing. She blinked, shaded her eyes, noted what appeared to be the top of a head barely visible above the back of the sofa.

With her heart pounding, she quietly crossed the room, walked around the sofa and nearly melted at what she saw. There was Rick Blaine, with orange stains on his shirt and spaghetti stuck to his hair, cradling the squeaky-clean, pajama-clad toddler in his arms. Both were sound asleep.

For a moment, Catrina just stood there gaping, unable to trust her own eyes. Never in her life had she seen anything that touched her so deeply. But then she'd never seen a man actually perform the role of father so naturally, so instinctively, with such loving reverence.

Intellectually, Catrina was well aware that there were such men in the world, men who nurtured children and who loved them. She'd just never witnessed it before, at least not in her own life.

This was the real Rick Blaine, she realized. Not the glib genius, not the brilliant bachelor, not the lonely man hiding behind the facade of friends. In one vulnerable, unguarded moment she had glimpsed the soul of a man who had the power to change her life forever. It was the worst thing that could happen. Because at that very same moment, Catrina fell utterly, completely and irrevocably in love. Her life would never, could never be the same.

Chapter Nine

"No, no, it's too big!"

"Relax, it's perfect. You'll love it."

"Are you trying to kill me? You are, you're trying to— Arghhh!" Catrina screamed as gravity flung her backward against Rick's chest, and the sled careened wildly down the snowy slope.

Whizzing past trees and truck-sized boulders, they spun down the hillside while Rick hollered, "Wheeeee!" with such joyous abandon that an onlooker would never realize that Catrina's entire life was flashing in front of her eyes.

A massive snow mound loomed in their path. They were heading right toward it, bouncing, sliding, speeding across the crusted snow on a piece of round, flat plastic no larger than a garbage-can lid.

"Hold on!" Rick shouted.

There was, of course, nothing for Catrina to hold

on to, except the frantic hope that there wasn't a boulder buried under that snow mound.

They hit with a splat. Catrina flipped once, landed on her stomach with her face buried in snow. Gasping for air, she flopped onto her back, saw Rick's flushed face looming over her.

"Are you all right?"

"I think so." She sucked a breath, narrowed her gaze. "No thanks to you."

He laughed, extended a hand to help her up. "Where's your adventurous spirit?"

"At the top of the hill, along with my stomach." She brushed snow off her pants, tried for a reproachful expression that she suspected didn't quite come off. "I told you it was too big."

"Come on, it was barely bigger than the bunny slope."

"I'm a bunny-slope kinda gal."

"Nobody is perfect." Chuckling, he bent to retrieve the circular plastic sled, then slipped an arm around Catrina's waist. "Besides, you have other appealing attributes."

"Hmm, tell me more." She lifted her face, waiting for his kiss, and was not disappointed. He kissed her sweetly, but so deeply that her knees wiggled, with a leashed passion that turned her bones to water and her blood to steam.

"Umm." Rick broke the kiss with obvious reluctance, nuzzled the corner of her mouth with gentle reverence. "I guess we'd better go find Gracie and Heather before they call out the rescue patrol."

"I suppose."

Catrina didn't want to leave this place of sweet

isolation any more than Rick did. In fact, she was sorely tempted to fling him into the snow and jump his bones right there under a weeping cedar. After all, she'd never made love in the snow before.

Actually she and Rick had never made love at all, but that had been due as much to his restraint as to hers. They'd never discussed sexual matters in so many words, but it was clear that both of them were cautious about expanding their relationship into that ultimate expression of intimacy.

Not that his desire hadn't been obvious. That he wanted her physically was never in question, yet he'd never placed her in the uncomfortable position of having to either submit or rebuff him. He seemed content merely to spend time with her. That quite frankly astounded her.

It had been three weeks since Catrina had found Rick asleep on her sofa, cuddling her slumbering child in his arms. Three of the most gloriously passionate weeks she'd ever experienced. Evenings were spent as a family, laughing over a burnt meat loaf, or hurrying through a fast-food dinner to watch a special movie on television.

Weekends had become mini-adventures, with a trip to the ocean to introduce Heather to the joys of sea foam licking her ankles, a leisurely stroll through the zoo while the wide-eyed toddler ogled funny monkeys, or just a lazy picnic in a nearby park. Rick had become an intricate part of Catrina's life. And of Heather's life, too.

The child clearly adored him.

One part of Catrina cherished that; another, more skeptical part of her warned that happiness was at best a fleeting thing. Nothing lasted forever, not even life itself.

Still, she couldn't deny herself the joy Rick brought, even as her heart ignored the warnings of her mind.

He scooped up the blue plastic sled, looped a proprietary arm around her shoulders. "Race you up the hill?"

"Run if you want, bucko, my toes are numb."

"Then the gallant thing for me to do would be to sweep you into my arms and carry you to civilization."

"Okay." She stopped in her tracks, held out her arms. "Take me, I'm yours."

His crestfallen expression was hilarious. "You really want me to carry you? Up a vertical slope the size of a six-story building?"

"I was told that this itsy-bitsy hill is barely bigger than a bunny slope, Mr. Gallant." She grinned smugly. "But I understand that the gesture was mere bravado. I'll let you off the hook this time."

"Dost thou imply a lack of masculine virtue, or the churlish drool of a man unable to protect his maiden from the ills of a cruel world?" He feigned an expression that was part astonishment, part indignation and totally amusing. "Nay, fair lass. No bravado this."

Still clasping the plastic disk in one hand, he bent forward as if to kiss her, but instead he slipped his free arm under her buttocks, gave a hefty heave, and before Catrina could refill her deflated lungs she was draped over his shoulder like the carcass of an unfortunate deer.

"To battle!" he bellowed, and charged up the hill with Catrina shrieking in protest.

By the time they reached the plateau beside the lodge where Gracie and Heather were making a snowman, Catrina was laughing so hard her stomach hurt, and Rick was panting like a man on the verge of collapse.

Gracie glanced up, did a double take and immediately dropped the handful of snow she'd just scooped up. "Good grief, call the paramedics."

Rick wheezed, bent forward until Catrina's feet touched the ground. "She's...okay," he said between gasps. "Just...cold...feet."

"Well you're certainly an expert on that topic," Gracie muttered. She stood, brushing loose snow from her mittened hands. "I know Catrina is okay, I was talking about you. Your face is turning gray."

"Probably just frostbite." Catching his breath, he straightened, dropped the plastic glider on the ground. "I was being gallant for m'lady, that's all."

"You were being a showoff," Catrina corrected. "Albeit an adorable one."

"It's not my fault that you're heavier than you look."

"Don't even go there."

"A tad touchy about our weight, are we?"

"Mention it again and you'll die ugly. Is that touchy enough for you?"

She playfully poked his shoulder, he grinned in response. Gracie just tossed up her hands and turned away, muttering to herself.

"Mommy, Mommy!" Heather scrambled to her

feet, bouncing with excitement. "Me make a snowman!"

"You did?" Catrina eyed the lopsided column topped by a lumpy protrusion that could charitably be considered some kind of skull formation. "And a fine-looking snowman it is, too."

Rick frowned, whispered from the corner of his mouth, "It seems a bit, umm, X-rated, don't you think? Maybe you'd better have a talk with your daughter."

"Behave yourself. She's only two, for heaven's sake."

"My mother isn't."

"You are terrible!"

Rick waggled his eyebrows, causing Catrina to snort back a laugh just as Heather stumbled toward them, so layered with clothing that she looked like a quilted ball with legs. The toddler flung herself against Rick's knees, arms extended upward with a series of grunts that needed no interpretation.

Rick automatically scooped the child up, allowed to her settle comfortably in the crook of his arm. "So what do you think of all this funny white stuff, little one?"

Heather's eyes widened. "I—I—I make a snowman!"

"And a fine figure of a snowman it is." The corner of Rick's mouth twitched only slightly. "Would you like to go for a sled ride?"

"Uh-huh!"

The baby bobbed her head, despite Catrina's immediate protest.

"You're not about to take her down that suicidal hill?"

"Nah, we'll stick with the real bunny slope." He sent her a grin, bent his knees to scoop up the plastic sled without dropping the child. "Like mother like daughter."

Catrina made a face at him, and he ambled off chuckling while Heather waved bye-bye over his shoulder.

They looked so natural together, Catrina thought. It was the way she'd always imagined a father-child relationship should be, although she'd only actually ever seen glimpses of it in the fathers of her childhood friends, or strangers interacting with their children.

When she'd been a child herself, Catrina had made up fantasies about her own absent father, creative stories about how he had been hunting and gathering to provide for his beloved family when aliens had swooped down from the sky, taking him to their own planet to study such a perfect example of loving human parenthood. He had, of course, spent the rest of his lonely life pining for his lost daughter, just as his lost daughter pined for him.

It was a tragic tale, but one which had offered her peculiar comfort. In some deep, faraway corner of her heart, part of her still wanted to believe that her father hadn't willingly left, just as her half sisters harbored the same secret wish about their own father's abandonment.

She wondered if Rick did, too.

And she wondered if these men realized how much emotional destruction they'd left in their wake. Perhaps they didn't understand what they'd done; or perhaps they simply didn't care.

"Do you still believe that love is a myth?"

The question startled her, partly because she hadn't realized Gracie was standing beside her and partly because she felt as if the woman must have some secret access to the sanctity of Catrina's private thoughts.

It took a moment to recall that she herself had made the "love is a myth" claim weeks earlier in Gracie's shop.

"Love is real enough," Catrina said quietly. "The myth is the mistaken belief that love, simply by virtue of its power, lasts forever."

Gracie considered that, her gaze locked on the handsome young man sledding down a shallow incline with a laughing toddler in his lap. "Forever is a long time."

"Yes." Catrina crossed her arms so tightly that the bones ached. "I'd settle for a few measly decades."

"That would certainly be nice." Tucking her hands in her jacket pocket, Gracie pursed her lips, rocked back on her heels. "I've always thought love was rather like an avocado. Most of the time it's too green to enjoy, yet if one is persistent enough, it will eventually ripen into soft, delicious perfection."

Catrina just stared at her. "Avocados also turn ugly when exposed to air, and are so perishable that they are only edible for a few hours before they go rancid and have to be thrown out."

"Ah, but anything so fragile and fleeting is all the more precious, is it not?"

"No," Catrina said with a frost to her voice she hadn't intended. "It is not. I hate avocados."

"Oh." Gracie shrugged. "Bad analogy, then." She brightened. "How do you feel about tomatoes?"

"I feel they have little to do with the complexity of human relationships."

"A stickler for reality, huh? Okay, let's cut to the chase. We both know that you're in love with my son. So what are you going to do about it?"

Taken aback by the woman's candor, Catrina tried for a light laugh that caught like a bone in her throat. She coughed it away, avoided Gracie's gaze, and managed a limp shrug. "I don't know."

"At least you're honest."

"I try to be." Catrina brushed a wet strand of hair out of her face. "And as you've so succinctly pointed out, I'm also a stickler for reality. I'm not the first woman to be charmed by your son. I doubt I'll be the last."

"What kind of attitude is that? If you want him, fight for him."

"Who am I supposed to fight? And what's the prize? A few more weeks or months with a man who wants to be free, and who will eventually leave anyway?" A crack in her voice betrayed the depth of her emotion. "We are enjoying each other's company at the moment, and that's fine with me."

"Is it?" Gracie studied her intently. "Well I must say, the two of you are cut from the same mold. I never thought I'd meet a woman as determined to avoid commitment as my own son, but life is full of surprises."

"I'm not determined to avoid commitment."

"What would you call it then?"

"A reality check." The topic was becoming more and more discomfiting, a stark reminder that happiness was fragile, fleeting. "Look Gracie, I'm not afraid of commitment. I've already made a big one, remember? I once vowed "till death do us part' to a man who walked out on me eleven months later. It's not my fault that my definition of the term doesn't seem to mesh with that of the rest of the world."

"The rest of the world?" Her smile was slightly sad, not unkind. "That's a lot of people."

To Catrina's horror, her stoicism crumbled. "I don't know what to do, Gracie. I promised myself that I'd never let my heart rule my head again, yet here I am, starry-eyed and filled with foolish fantasies that I know are doomed from the start. Why am I doing this to myself? What's wrong with me?"

Gracie slipped a warm arm around her shoulder. "Nothing is wrong with you, dear. You are a perfectly normal young woman who has fallen in love with a perfectly normal young man. It happens every day."

Moist heat gathered in her eyes, infuriating her. "I don't want to lose him, Gracie, and yet I know that sooner or later he'll move on. He always has, he always will. It's who he is, a man who requires new faces, new friends, new experiences in his life. Right now, Heather and I represent a new experience. Eventually he'll tire of us, and when that happens, I'm not sure how I'll be able to deal with it."

"Do you honestly believe that? If so, I'm surprised you could fall in love with a man you think so callow."

Catrina considered her response carefully. "Rick isn't a callow man, Gracie, you of all people know that. He is, however, a unique individual, a person who fears the loss of freedom beyond all else."

The woman heaved a troubled sigh. "It's not the loss of freedom my son fears. It's the loss of those he has allowed himself to love." She angled a glance. "I'm sure you understand that fear, since you share it."

Such insight was disturbing, to say the least. Catrina stiffened her shoulders, as if the gesture could put some distance between her dear friend's unnerving perception and her own silent turmoil. "It's human nature to fear losing the people we love, Gracie."

"Of course it is." Recognizing the mute request for distance, Gracie removed her arm from Catrina's shoulder. "But denying ourselves the joy of love as a protective measure isn't the answer."

A chill slipped down Catrina's spine. "What is the answer?"

"Only God knows that, child. But He gave you a fine mind and a trusting heart for a reason. Don't ignore His gifts. Use them as He intended."

"In other words, don't look for trouble, let nature take its course?"

Gracie shrugged. "Would that be so bad?"

Catrina didn't respond, was vaguely aware that Gracie had left, although the question she'd posed continued to haunt Catrina.

Would it really be so bad to live for the moment, to enjoy today without constantly worrying about what tomorrow might bring? Throughout her life

Catrina had always focused both eyes firmly on the future, had made every major decision based on avoiding worst-case scenarios at all costs.

It had seemed a mature, thoughtful approach to an unpredictable world. If she couldn't control the pain of living, couldn't she at least mitigate the extent of damage? It had seemed a reasonable alternative to the agony of constant heartbreak. Perhaps it was simply a coward's shield.

A few yards away, Rick was trudging up a snowy slope with Heather in his arms. Both were wet, shivering, laughing as if they didn't have a care in the world. Even from this distance Catrina could see how tightly the toddler's arms were wrapped around Rick's neck, how possessively her tiny fingers grasped the collar of his jacket. Happiness glowed in the twist of her giggly grin, the pink radiance of her cheeks.

Catrina's own heart ached with gratitude. The joy in her child's face was a wonder, a blessing. Perhaps even a curse.

The dichotomous thought took her by surprise. She realized that Gracie was right, she did have a tendency to dissect good into molecules of potential pain. Catrina had ruined so many happy moments in her own life that way; she was determined not to ruin her child's happiness as well.

"You're a curly-headed speed demon." Exhausted, Rick rolled onto his back in the snow, while the persistent toddler yanked on his hand.

"More," she whined. "Wanna go again."

"Have you no mercy? I am old and breakable."

"Uh-uh." Heather's frown morphed into a mischievous grin a moment before the toddler flung herself onto Rick's chest, unceremoniously deflating his lungs with a single whoosh. "Wanna go, wanna go!"

Rick would have responded if he hadn't been busy trying to breathe, a process that might have been considerably easier if the toddler hadn't been bouncing on his rib cage.

"Rick?" A shadow fell over them. "Rick Blaine?"

Wheezing, Rick tried to focus on the vaguely familiar man looming above him. Since he couldn't speak, he simply nodded and gulped air.

Heather, struck by a sudden shyness, scrambled off his chest and lurked a short distance away, chewing her mittened fingers.

Rick rolled onto his side, refilling his lungs and gaining enough strength to squint into the grinning face of Jason Montgomery, a fellow he now recalled having met a couple of years ago when they'd been competing for the same project. Rick had garnered the job, but just barely.

Jason rocked back, laughing. "Holy smokes, Blaine, I thought I was keeping up with all the industry gossip, but I never heard a thing about you giving up your bachelor ways." He extended a hand, helped Rick to his feet. "A lovely child, Rick. You must be very proud."

"Oh, she's not mine." The speed and force of his reply surprised Rick. He didn't know why the assumption that he'd fathered a child was disconcerting, but for some reason he couldn't quite identify why he'd felt compelled to set the record straight without delay.

He glanced at Heather, who still had her fingers hooked in her drooling mouth and was eyeing this stranger with wary interest. Something softened inside him. Instinctively, he shored it up. "The baby belongs to a friend, that's all."

"A friend." Jason's eyes gleamed, but he merely shrugged a shoulder. "I should have known that the world's most determined bachelor wouldn't have been shot down without making headlines. My apologies for the premature presumption."

Heather sidled behind Rick to clutch the back of his legs. She peered out from behind his thigh, offered Jason a devastating baby grin.

Jason grinned back. "Well, hello there. What's your name?"

Heather giggled, hid her face.

"Heather," came a frosty reply from behind Rick. "Her name is Heather."

Rick barely had time to turn around before Catrina scooped the baby into her arms. She spared Rick a glance before turning her attention to Jason. "I'm Catrina Jordan, Rick's 'friend.'"

The emphasis on that final word and the coolness with which it was issued made Rick flinch. He was vaguely aware that Jason had finished the introduction.

"It's nice to meet you, Mr. Montgomery." Catrina shifted the baby in her arms, avoided Rick's gaze. "I hope you'll excuse us. My daughter has had about all the excitement she can take for one day. She needs to rest now."

"Of course," Jason replied politely, even though he was speaking to the back of Catrina's head as she marched away.

Jason watched with a bemused expression. "I'm no expert on women, since I've only been married for nine years. But if I were a betting man, I'd wager that young lady is not pleased with you at the moment."

"That's a sucker bet," Rick muttered. He wasn't too sure what he'd done, but whatever it was, Rick had sure as heck done it wrong.

The drive home was strained, with conversation that was too careful, too polite, and tension thick enough to slice. At first Gracie gamely attempted to keep up a stream of inane chatter. After a while, she gave up, gazing out the back window while Heather snoozed beside her in her car seat.

They dropped Gracie off first, then drove to Catrina's apartment a couple of blocks away. Rick had tried to retrieve the sleeping toddler from the car seat, only to have Catrina take her from him.

Now Catrina tucked the baby into her crib, wondering if Rick would still be in the living room when she returned.

He was.

He rose from the sofa as she entered, clicked the remote to turn off the television. Beside him, his thick jacket was wadded in a heap, as if he wanted it close enough to grab in a hurry.

Catrina moistened her lips, twisted her fingers together. "Would you like some coffee or hot chocolate?"

"No thanks."

An awkward silence stretched between them. "Something stronger? I have beer in the fridge."

"No, I'm fine. Really." He sighed, raked his hair with his fingers. "Actually, I'm not fine at all. I've annoyed you somehow, haven't I?"

Catrina swallowed hard, focused on a thin settling crack in the corner of the wall. "I'm not annoyed with you, Rick. I'm annoyed with myself."

"I don't understand."

That didn't surprise her, since she barely understood it herself. "When you look into your own future, a year or two years from now, what exactly do you see for yourself, for your life?"

He stared at her as if she'd sprouted antlers. "I don't really know, I've never actually thought about it."

It was the answer she'd expected from him. "That's the main difference between us, you know. You never think about the future, and I can't seem to think about anything else."

Perhaps it was a trick of the light, but he seemed a bit paler than he'd been moments before. "Nobody knows what the future will bring. It's a waste of energy trying to decipher the impossible."

"That's not your position on fiscal forecasting. I happen to know that you're a real stickler on five-year-projection reports."

"That's business."

"Business is just another form of life. You plan for your business, but your personal life is based on the live-for-the-moment theory."

"So, what's wrong with that?"

"Nothing, really. It's just not...me." Hot moisture seeped into her eyes, annoying her. She swiped it away. "When I was about three my mother and father got into a terrible fight. It was over me. My babysitter had a family emergency, and my mother had to go to work, so she wanted my father to watch me. It was his bowling night, so he was not pleased."

The memory swelled back like a phantom from the past, swirling around her with vivid images once forgotten. She didn't look at Rick, although she was aware that he was listening attentively.

"The details elude me," she whispered, "but I do recall him bringing me to the bowling alley, sitting me on a bench and never speaking to me the entire night. Some of his friends tried to be nice. They asked if I was hungry or thirsty. My father told them to mind their own business, that I had to toughen up and get used to being on my own." She hugged herself, managed a limp shrug. "Two days later he was gone. I never saw him again."

Silence fell around her like a shroud. Across the room, Rick tucked his thumbs in his pockets, eyed her with more wariness than empathy. "That's a very sad story," he said carefully. "Something like that should never happen to a child, any child."

"That's right, it shouldn't. And I'm going to do everything in my power to make sure it doesn't happen to my child, even if it means depriving her of happiness now to keep her from being hurt in the future."

"I don't know what you mean," he said, although his eyes quite clearly reflected that he did. "I would never be unkind to Heather, or hurt her in any way. I...care deeply for her."

"I know you do. But what my daughter needs, you can't give her." Catrina took a shuddering breath, faced him squarely. "I don't want my daughter to love you, Rick. Sooner or later you'll leave her, and the loss will be devastating."

It wasn't a trick of the light. Rick was white as a snowbank, and looked as if he might faint. "What exactly are you asking me to do? Marry you?"

Her own skin turned icy. "I would never ask such a thing, not from you or any man."

"But is that what you want?"

"Marriage isn't the answer. I thought it was once, but I quickly learned that a piece of paper does not a lifetime commitment make."

"Nobody can make a lifetime commitment, Catrina, nobody who doesn't have a crystal ball and a direct pipeline to God. It's a fool's quest." His voice was slightly ragged, a little desperate. "You want the impossible, a guarantee that everything will always stay exactly as it is now, that individuals won't grow and evolve, that circumstances will never change. People don't have that kind of control over their lives, Catrina. We'd like to think we do, but we don't."

"I know that," she whispered. "Dear Lord, I know that only too well."

"You can't protect your daughter from disappointment."

"I can try."

"Even if it means taking away anything that might make her happy just because it may not make her happy forever?" He stepped toward her, jerked to a stop, swaying as if being pulled in two directions at the same time. "I don't understand that."

"Yes, you do, Rick. Sadly, you understand all too well. That's why you are so averse to commitment—you've experienced the heartache of broken promises and shattered families."

When he visibly shuddered, Catrina realized that she'd hit a nerve.

She softened her tone. "We're not so different, you and I. We both avoid things that cause us pain, situations we can't control. The main difference is that you are in the enviable position of making those decisions based only on how they affect you personally. I have to make them based on how they affect my child."

His expression was one of stunned defeat. "I guess I have no choice but to accept that." He plucked his jacket off the sofa, spent a moment smoothing it while his mind was clearly elsewhere, then spun on his heel and strode to the front door.

She stopped him when he reached for the knob. "Rick?"

He paused, looked over his shoulder.

"I love you," she whispered.

An expression of exquisite pain flashed through his eyes. "I know you do."

And then he was gone.

Chapter Ten

"Does the term *self-fulfilling prophecy* mean anything to you?"

"Hmm?" Catrina blinked, glanced up from the mental reverie into which she'd submerged herself for an unspecified amount of time.

It took a moment to reorient to her surroundings, the familiar scents of lilac and jasmine from the potpourri candles Gracie favored, to the theme music thrumming behind the credits of the video that had apparently run its course. That Catrina couldn't even recall what film they'd been watching was somewhat shocking.

It was, after all, Mel Gibson night.

Across the room, Gracie cradled the sleeping toddler in her arms. "Allow me to define the term. A self-fulfilling prophecy is one in which the seer deliberately creates the predicted destiny in order to satisfy a narcissistic sense of 'I told you so.'"

A dull throb spread behind Catrina's eyebrows. She set aside the bowl of cold, uneaten popcorn that she'd apparently been clutching for the past two hours. "You promised we wouldn't discuss my private life."

"I lied."

Catrina crossed the room, popped the tape from the VCR. "I didn't have any choice, Gracie. Heather was becoming too attached to Rick."

"So naturally you had to nip that in the bud." The woman glanced down to assure herself that the baby was still sleeping soundly, then spoke in a quiet voice to avoid awakening her. "You know I think the world of you, dear, but preventing your child from forming attachments under the guise of protecting her from potential disappointment will only stunt her ability to distinguish positive influences on her life from negative ones. You can't wrap her up in a bubble, and keep her alone for the rest of her life."

"That's not fair, Gracie."

"Life isn't fair." She sighed, carefully shifted the slumbering child to the sofa, then stood and crossed the room to embrace Catrina. "At least be honest with yourself, dear. You were terribly wounded as a child, and I don't doubt that you would do anything, even walk through fire, to keep your own child from suffering as you did. I know that you sincerely believe you're protecting her. The truth is that you're protecting yourself."

Denial rolled to the tip of Catrina's tongue, and stuck there. It was true, she realized. As devastated as she'd been by her father's abandonment, the starkest pain had been witnessing her mother's agony.

And feeling personally responsible for it.

A lump of misery wedged in Catrina's throat. "I always believed that Daddy left because of me, because I was too annoying, too demanding, because I ate too much, wore out my clothes too fast, took up too much of his time. Every time I heard my mother crying behind her bedroom door, I felt like her suffering was all my fault."

Gracie nodded, squeezed her shoulders. "I understand that. To a lesser extent, Rick had to deal with exactly the same thing. That's why the two of you are constantly circling each other, holding shields over your hearts. If either of you were simply willing to disarm, and take a chance...."

Her voice trailed off. Dropping her arms to her side, she turned away, wiped her face with her hands. She looked so weary, Catrina realized, so emotionally drained.

"I'm sorry," Gracie said finally. "If I sound like an advocate for my son, well, I suppose it's because I am. You're right about him, and the truth is frequently painful." She straightened, glanced over her shoulder. "Rick is a wonderful man, perhaps one of the finest men I've ever known. I'm so proud of him I could burst. But he doesn't see in himself what others see. Rick looks in the mirror, and his father's reflection looks back at him. He doesn't believe in love, doesn't believe in commitment. That's my fault, I'm afraid. The failures in my life have had such a profound effect on him."

Catrina was stunned. "You can't take responsibility for choices made by others."

"Why not? You do."

The trap had been so expertly set that Catrina was

completely ensnared before she realized what had happened. "It's not the same thing, Gracie."

"And the differences are?"

"The differences are—" Catrina stumbled over her tongue. "—different," she finished lamely.

"Ah. That clarifies everything." Gracie shrugged. "The point is moot anyway. Real love doesn't rely on a long-term-commitment forecast to justify its existence. Love cherishes each moment as a gift without demanding guarantees. Love is its own reward. To deny oneself love because it may not last forever is akin to denying oneself life because death is the inevitable outcome."

Catrina was trembling, chilled to the bone. Every word Gracie spoke struck a mortal blow to the facade of logic meticulously erected to defend the indefensible. "I'm just so frightened," she whispered.

Gracie's eyes softened with empathy. She opened her arms, and Catrina fell into her motherly embrace. "Shh, I know, dear. Handing over a hunk of our heart is pretty scary stuff. There are no guarantees that it will be handled with care."

That was the crux of the matter in a nutshell. Hearts were so fragile. Little hearts, big hearts, all vulnerable to crippling wounds, injury by indifference. Eventually self-protection becomes all-consuming, and wounded become wounders.

"It's too late," Catrina whispered.

"Nonsense, it's never too late to communicate openly with the people we care about." Gracie sighed, stepped away, pursing her lips in thoughtful contemplation. "I know Rick has been in Vancouver the past few days, but when he returns I'm sure the two of you will run into each other in a hallway, or your eyes will meet across a crowded conference table. Once you've both had a chance to clear your minds, think things through more rationally—"

"It's too late for that." Catrina wiped her eyes, turned away in abject misery. "I quit my job yesterday. Heather and I will be moving to Bakersfield at the end of the month."

Gracie stumbled back as if she'd been slapped. "You can't be serious. What on earth is in Bakersfield?"

It was more a question of what wasn't there, or rather who wasn't there. "I've been offered a job, and the cost of living is lower in that area, which makes it easier for single parents to survive." Catrina could not meet Gracie's gaze. "I'm sorry. I know how much you'll miss Heather, and how much she'll miss you. But I can't stay, don't you see? Every time I see him, every time I catch a whiff of his scent in the hallway I just fall apart inside."

Gracie's eyes reddened. She turned away with a sniff, her shoulders rigid, her spine straight as an arrow. "I wish you well, dear. Keep in touch."

There was a finality in Grace's tone, an acceptance of the inevitable that chilled Catrina to the bone. It really was too late. And both women knew it.

Nursing his second straight Scotch of the evening, Rick rotated the warm glass between his palms, tried not to eavesdrop on the conversation across the table.

It was difficult not to overhear, however, since Frank Glasgow had never been accused of speaking softly in any forum, and had a tendency to raise his voice while on the phone as if trying to circumvent the primary purpose of such technology.

"Yes, yes, my schedule is clear that weekend," he said loudly enough to raise eyebrows around the Vancouver hotel bar. Frank tucked his appointment book back into the breast pocket of his suit coat. "Tell Sandy and Bart we'll be glad to watch the children.... Hmm?... Oh, that shouldn't be a problem." He chuckled, shifted the cell phone to his left ear. "Remind them that we managed to raise four of our own without slitting our wrists or their throats. I suspect we can muddle through without an instruction sheet."

Rick leaned back, took a healthy swallow of bitter liquid and winced as it burned its way down his throat. Now if it would only numb his mind, he'd be a happy man. Life was a constant challenge with the image of a certain brown-eyed blonde floating through his mind every minute of every hour of every damned day.

There ought to be a law against worming one's way into a man's head. Into his heart.

Ought to be a law.

He drained his drink with a single swallow, held the empty glass up to capture the server's attention. The smiling young man nodded, hustled off to the bar for a refill.

"I'm not sure, sweetheart," Frank said. "Rick keeps extending our visit. He's added two more introductory meetings with city officials tomorrow, and a conference with the local architectural committee the day after." Frank angled a pointed glance across the table, although Rick pretended not to notice. The disgruntled finance director returned to the phone conversation with a loud and not-so-jovial chuckle. "On the bright side, if we ever wish to apply for dual citizenship I suspect our Canadian residency requirements will already have been met."

Rick dug into his pocket, handed a bill to the server who'd returned with a fresh drink. "Just bring me the bottle and a straw," he muttered. "It's going to be a long night."

The smiling server ambled away.

Frank finally thumbed off the cell phone, and tucked it in his pocket. "Lucille says I am to be on the next plane to Los Angeles, and if you give me grief she suggests I tape your mouth shut and strap you to the wing."

"Cute." Rick tipped his glass, felt the burn. "I hope your next boss has a sense of humor."

"My wife misses me. Is that so difficult to believe?"

"Not difficult, damned near impossible. I hadn't realized how annoying it can be to spend nearly 24-7 with someone who rings my room at 6:00 a.m. because he doesn't like to eat breakfast alone."

"We had an eight o'clock meeting, and if you hadn't insisted on closing the bar the previous night, you might actually have had something worthwhile to contribute to that gathering of potential clients besides, 'who has an aspirin?' and 'my tongue needs a shave.'"

Rick flinched. All right, so it hadn't been his finest hour. Everyone was entitled to an off-day once in a while. "At least my cell phone didn't go off three times because the family couldn't decide what to thaw for dinner."

Frank shrugged, smiled. "My youngest son had just been announced class valedictorian. That's certainly worth a phone call. And one of my grandchildren broke his ankle playing Batman in the backyard tree. A grandfather must know these things. Oh, and the final call was from my wife, who simply missed me and wanted to hear my voice."

"Which she hadn't heard for at least two hours, since you've never gone longer than that without yanking out the damned phone just to hear about the soap opera she's watching." The bitter edge on his voice startled him to his toes. He straightened, set his glass down. "I'm sorry, Frank. You know I adore Lucille. I have no idea why in hell I even said such a thing."

Frank shrugged, motioned for the server to bring another glass of white wine. "Envy tends to make a person testy."

"You think I envy you?"

"I think you envy what I have, Rick. I've seen the look in your eyes when I call my family, or when they call me. It's not a resentful expression, or even an angry one. It's the doleful gaze of a man wishing his own phone would ring."

"My phone rings day and night, thank you."

"Ah, but it's not the process of ringing that matters so much as who is making the call in the first place." Frank paused long enough to signal the server for another glass of white wine. "Family is the glue that supports us, unites us, makes us part of something larger than ourselves. Most people crave that. Certainly you do, which is why you treat your business like a family and your employees like relatives."

A chill ran down Rick's spine. "Thank you, Dr. Ruth."

"There's nothing wrong with it, of course. That

family atmosphere is what gives Blaine Architectural such a pleasant working environment. But it's not a realistic substitute for the real thing."

"I treat people nicely," Rick snapped. "That doesn't make me neurotic."

Frank merely smiled. He wasn't one to be intimidated by a show of bluster, even from a man with the power to fire him. "You're not neurotic, just a bit of an emotional coward. Not that I blame you, given your chaotic youth, but that was then, and this is now." When the server approached, Frank paused long enough to retrieve the glass of wine, then raised it in Rick's direction. "Let the past go, Rick. If you don't, it'll strangle your future."

Rick would have made a scathing retort if he could have thought of one. Unfortunately, Frank was right. He was frequently right, although arrogant enough in his correctness that it galled Rick to acknowledge it openly.

Still he was one of the few people Rick could count on to provide the unvarnished truth about any given situation, regardless of how unpleasant or politically incorrect said truth might be.

Frank set his wineglass down, leaned his elbows on the table. "Call her, Rick. Just swallow your wounded pride, pick up the phone and tell her how you feel."

The room was beginning to blur nicely. A fuzzy warmth seeped into his bones but stubbornly refused to numb the ache in his chest. He took another sip of his drink, regarded the man across from him with a deep-rooted trust few in Rick's life had ever managed to garner. "How can I tell Catrina how I feel when I don't even know myself?"

"You know. It frightens you, but you know."

Rick flinched. "Damn it, Frank, your candor gets old after a while."

"So I've been told." Leaning back, he shifted in the chair to cross his legs, slipped his fingers around the stem of the wineglass and held it as if it were a brandy snifter. "Unless I am very much mistaken, which I rarely am, mind you, your feelings for the young woman in question will not disappear any time soon, regardless of how much you'd like them to. Since you are a miserable SOB to work with when you're befuddled by matters of the heart, I've been elected by our colleagues to insist that you resolve the situation immediately."

"Catrina dumped me. How am I supposed to resolve that?"

"Women don't normally dump men they are in love with unless they have an exceptionally good reason to do so. What was hers?"

A nervous cough took Rick by surprise. It gave him the luxury of an extra moment to consider his response. "She had the best reason in the world. She wants a man who can be a good father to her child, and she knows that isn't me."

"How does she know that?"

Rick shrugged. "I told her so."

"Ah."

"Don't look at me like that. It's true. I'd make a lousy father."

"Precisely how are fathers 'made,' Rick? Beyond the obvious scenario of actually being thrust in the position of caring for and nurturing offspring."

A fine question, one to which Rick actually had a fine answer. "Fatherhood must be learned, of course, and to be learned it must be taught. I don't know what it takes to be a good father, because no one ever showed me what a father does." Rick noticed the hike of Frank's brow and read beyond it. "You're a good father, Frank. Be honest, you had a good father as a role model, right?"

"Indeed I did. Poppa was a taskmaster, but a fine man who taught all of his seven children by example."

Rick tossed back another swallow of Scotch. "There you have it."

"My father, however, was not as blessed as were his children. He was orphaned as a toddler, during the days when crowded orphanages kept children like cattle, then kicked them onto the street at puberty with little more than the clothes on their back." Frank paused long enough for that scenario to sink in. "He had no parental role model of either gender. He was left to survive basically on his own, without ever experiencing parental love, nurture or support. When he had children of his own, he did not draw from his own role models, since none had ever been available. Instead, he instilled in his children a strength of purpose and values adopted from his own hard-fought life lessons."

Rick squirmed, frowned. "It sounds as if your father was exceptional."

"No doubt about that. What made him exceptional, however, was his refusal to submit to self-imposed restrictions based on deprivations of youth. Since he'd been rejected all his life, he could have chosen to reject others, thus protecting himself from future pain. Instead, he drew upon what he himself had endured as a basis to nurture his own children with an understanding of the human spirit that was profound indeed." Frank's eyes warmed with empathy. "Falling in love isn't usually something any of us plan, Rick. It's traumatic, a violent overthrow of one's heart and in many cases, one's soul. It can be bitter, it can be beautiful, it can purge and purify, it can harden and disappoint. But it is the most hallowed of human emotions, and life without it is always less than it could otherwise be."

Something cracked deep inside Rick. A fluid warmth spread through his veins, pumping with every heartbeat until his entire body felt as if it glowed. Perhaps the effects of the liquor had finally kicked in, or perhaps it was simply that for the first time in his life he had, in a small way, experienced the sage counsel of father to son.

Frank had given him that gift, taken him under his parental wing, and offered him the role model Rick had so desperately sought. "I hope your own kids realize how lucky they are."

"They could use a reminder."

"I'll see to it personally." Rick hesitated, met his friend's gaze directly. "Thank you."

"For what?"

"For being a good enough friend to treat me like a son."

"My next step was to send you to your room. You might not have thanked me for that." His grin widened. "On the other hand, I sense this might be an opportune time to ask for a raise."

Rick smiled.

A cold drizzle had turned into an icy, pouring rain. The windshield wipers struggled under the deluge, ineffective but insistent.

Catrina slowed the car to a crawl, squinting through the watery blur for the driveway into the apartment building's flooded parking lot. She saw it, made the turn, managed to pull into her space without drowning the engine.

An umbrella was out of the question, since she needed both hands to bundle Heather under a blanket for the mad dash to her front door. She retrieved the toddler, ducked into the whipping wind, and sloshed blindly through the storm.

She barely saw the hunched figure on her porch before she tripped over him.

Rick stood instantly. He was soaked to the skin, with rain pouring in rivulets from his soggy hair to run down a face twisted in pain.

Catrina's breath caught in her throat. "You're wet," she said stupidly.

"Yeah." He jammed his hands in his jacket pocket, an automatic response he frequently used to buy himself time. "You are, too." He flinched, apparently not pleased with the brilliant response those few seconds had purchased. "I, ah...should move so you can get the baby inside."

With that, he stepped away, allowing her access to the door. The keys were clutched in her icy fingers, and she fumbled several unlocking attempts.

Rick stepped forward, slipped his hand over hers. The warmth of his touch made her shiver even harder. She didn't know why.

Or maybe she did.

"Let me," he said softly.

She relinquished the keys, and a moment later they stood in the living room, dripping all over the carpet.

He stepped around one of the half-filled packing cartons dotting the living room. There was a haunted look in his eyes.

"I, ah..." She swallowed. "Just let me get these wet clothes off Heather, and I'll get you a towel."

"Sure." He studied a stack of framed photographs that had once hung on the living-room wall, but were now piled on the coffee table, waiting to be packed. "No problem."

"You wet!" Heather said with a gleeful squeak. "Me got new boots!"

His gaze warmed with his smile. "And fine looking boots they are. Do you like the rain?"

"Uh-huh." The toddler frowned as Catrina tugged off her jacket, then sat her on the floor to tug off the boots of which she was so proud. "No, my boots, *my* boots!"

Please God, Catrina prayed silently, *don't let her have a tantrum.* "We only wear rain boots outside, sweetie, and only when it's raining. We have to take them off now."

"No!" The baby shrieked, threw herself backward and began to flail her arms while kicking wildly to prevent Catrina from removing her beloved boots.

If humiliation were fatal, Catrina would have expired on the spot. "Heather, honey," she said through gritted teeth. "You don't want a time out while we have company, do you?"

Tears leaked from Heather's eyes, mingling with droplets of rainwater on her red cheeks. She sucked a breath, then emitted a wail loud enough to stop traffic three blocks away.

Catrina was horrified. She scooped up the thrashing child, hustled her into the bedroom and put her in the crib. Tantrums like this weren't routine, but they weren't unheard of either. The only way Catrina had found to deal with them was to remove Heather from the situation until she'd calmed down.

Of course, she managed to get the boots off first.

When Catrina returned to the living room, Rick was still where she'd left him, his eyes huge, his hands still jammed into the pockets of his dripping jacket. "She really likes those boots, doesn't she?"

"Not as much as she likes to dish out an occasional reminder of who is really boss around here."

"You handled it quite—" he flinched as Heather's angry shrieks from the bedroom rose another decibel "—well."

"Now you know the truth," she said with a tight laugh. "All those gooey stories parents tell about their adorable children are simply vengeful lies designed to sucker others into sharing the misery."

A series of thuds reverberated through the apartment. Rick's eyes nearly popped out of his head. "Good Lord, what is that?"

"She's kicking the crib slats," Catrina said. "She does that when her throat starts to get sore, but she's not quite ready to give up."

"This is...normal?"

She leveled her gaze, studied him without flinching. "It is for Heather, and for most two-year-olds, I'll wager. Children test their limits. It's what they do to study the world, and discover their own place in it." Catrina regarded his stunned expression, and felt as if she might burst into tears herself. He looked so bewildered, so utterly unnerved. It hurt her, yet it also touched her. There was something innately appealing about his confusion, something endearing about the fact that despite his obvious discomfort, he hadn't run away screaming. "At this point you must be thanking your lucky stars for a lifetime membership to the honorable institution of confirmed bachelorhood."

The teasing comment had been designed to lighten the mood, express a subtle understanding of how alien this must seem to him. But to her horror, her voice cracked, and she sounded as if she was about to cry.

Blinking rapidly, she turned her back on him, heard herself stutter. "Where are my manners? Would you like some coffee...?" Her gaze fell on the vacant kitchen counter. "I guess I've already packed the coffeemaker. I can heat a cup of water in the microwave—"

He interrupted. "Why are you leaving?"

Every drop of moisture evaporated from her mouth. "It's best."

"Best for whom?"

"Best for everybody."

He fell silent. Catrina forced herself not to look over her shoulder, knowing that she'd crumble emotionally at even the merest glimpse of regret in his eyes.

When he spoke again, his voice was soft, a feather of sound brushing past the pounding of the rain, and the angry wails of a thwarted child. "I don't want to lose you."

Catrina moistened her lips, glanced toward the hallway door through which Heather's fading sobs still echoed. "Accounting clerks are a dime a dozen.

Frank will probably have a replacement there before the end of the week."

"I'm not talking about the job."

The rustle of wet fabric announced that he was on the move. She didn't have to look to know that he was standing close behind her now, close enough that his scent enveloped her like a sweet embrace. Instinctively she knew that he was going to touch her. If he did, she would be lost.

"Don't," she whispered. "If you've come to say goodbye, let's just say it and go on with our lives."

"I don't want to say goodbye, Catrina. As for going on with our lives, all I know is that my own life will be a sad and lonely place if you and Heather are not a part of it."

She turned and looked at him then. It was a mistake. There was no teasing smile, no sparkle of humor in his eyes to reveal that he was joking. His expression was humble, his gaze mirrored in misery.

"I've never been in love," he said quietly. "I honestly didn't think it really existed outside of maudlin movies and romance novels. I believed it to be merely a figure of speech to justify why perfectly rational humans made a conscious choice to give up most of their autonomy and all of their freedom. It made a certain legal sense, I suppose, when one's yearning for genetic immortality spurred those reproductive urges, but it certainly wasn't for me."

A sharp pain shifted from her stomach to the center of her chest. "You've been very clear on that point."

"Yes, I have." The bitter edge on his voice startled her. "Good old Rick, everybody's friend, bachelor of the year, can't fault the fellow's honesty."

He sighed, wiped his face with his hands. "God, I can't even do this right."

"Do what?" Concerned, Catrina automatically laid a hand on his arm.

Rick grabbed it as if it were a lifeline, pressed her palm to his cheek. "Bear with me. I've never done this before." Something in his eyes held her silent. He took a deep breath. "You do not need me in your life. I know that. But I have discovered that I need you, Catrina, need you more than I would have ever thought possible. If you tell me to go, I will. And I'll survive, but it won't really be living. Because a part of me will be missing, the best part, the part that I've given to you." He kissed her fingertips, pressed her palm against his chest. "What do you feel?"

She swallowed hard. "A cold, wet jacket?"

"Exactly. And behind that cold, wet jacket is half a heart, struggling to beat as if it were whole." He gazed down at her hand, caressed it with his thumb. "You have the other half, Catrina, you and Heather. Don't bother trying to return it. You own it now. It's yours forever."

"Forever is a long time," Catrina whispered. "Things change. People change."

He shook his head. "I can't dispute that, but I can say that no matter what occurs, no matter what our future brings, I want to be a part of your life, Catrina, your entire life. I want to sleep with you in my arms, wake up with you beside me until you are gray and frail and I am bald and paunchy and we go through more diapers than our grandchildren." He flushed at her startled laugh. "Not a very romantic image, I know. I told you I wasn't very good at this."

She caressed his chin with her index finger. "Actually, I think it's just about the most romantic thing anyone has ever said to me."

A flash of relief illuminated his eyes, followed immediately by a veil of caution. "I don't know how to be a husband, honey, and I sure as hell don't know how to be a father. The truth is that I can't think of a single reason why you would want to spend your life with a man who is, according to a very wise friend of mine, an 'emotional coward.'"

Catrina smiled. "What a coincidence. A wise friend of mine said that if either one of us would just disarm and take a chance...well, she didn't finish the sentence. I think perhaps we're finishing it for her."

"Sounds like something my mother would say." Rick took a breath, exhaled slowly, held up his hands. "I'm disarmed, just as I was the first day I laid eyes on you and knew my life would never be the same." He hesitated. "How about you, Catrina? Shall we take that chance, and make my mother the happiest grandma on earth?"

Catrina regarded him for a moment. "That depends."

"On what?"

"On you, Rick. You said yourself that you can't think of a single, solitary reason why I would want to spend my life with you."

He paled slightly. "There is one reason."

"I'm listening."

He coughed, shifted his feet, looked as if the words had clogged in his throat. "The baby has stopped crying," he blurted.

Catrina's heart sank like a rock. "It's past her nap time. She's probably fallen asleep."

"Oh. Sure. Kids do that." He swallowed, his gaze darting as if seeking escape.

Just when Catrina was certain he'd bolt from the room, his demeanor changed completely. His stiff shoulders relaxed, the color returned to his face, his eyes warmed and his lips curved into a smile. "I love you, Catrina. I've never said those words to anyone before, never even understood what they truly meant, but I do now. I love you with every breath in my body, every fiber of my soul. I can't promise what tomorrow will bring, or the day after, or next month or next year. But I can promise that I will never leave you unless you kick me out the door and lock it behind me. And I will never, ever stop loving you."

Tears sprang to her eyes. "Never is a long time."

"Not nearly long enough," he whispered. "But it's a start."

Epilogue

A lazy surf splayed foamy fingers between pier pylons encrusted with barnacles. The beach was crowded as usual, but not exceptionally so considering the delicious warmth of yet another lovely spring day.

Catrina shaded her eyes, smiling to herself. There he was, tanned and virile, his broad shoulders bared to the sun, and glistening with moisture. Her heart still raced at the sight of him, still ached with emotion at the stunning realization that she had actually been Mrs. Rick Blaine for nearly two years.

"You'd better put some lotion on your legs, dear. You don't want to burn."

"Hmm?" Offering a sideways glance, Catrina smiled at the dear woman who had become such an intrinsic part of her life, and of her children's lives. "I'm wearing a T-shirt and a pair of knee shorts,

Gracie. I think the few inches of skin I'm actually revealing can stand a bit of sunshine."

Shifting her six-week-old granddaughter in her arms, Gracie clucked her tongue in that delightfully maternal manner Catrina had become so dependent upon. "A bit of a tummy pouch is normal after childbirth, Catrina. As svelte as you are, there's no reason to bury yourself in floppy clothing." She covered the baby's face with the corner of a receiving blanket, angled a quizzical glance. "Unless my son has been criticizing your figure? Has he? If so, I'll turn him over my knee this instant."

Stunned even by the question, Catrina laughed out loud. "Rick is the most devoted husband imaginable. He didn't even appear to notice that during the final months of pregnancy my belly stuck out like a mutant watermelon, and I walked like a penguin on greased ice. What makes you think he'd care about a bit of temporary tummy flab?"

"Well, your outfit for one thing."

"Pure ego. Mine, not his. I tried on my favorite two-piece suit this morning. The result was not pretty." She chuckled, raised her sunglasses to prop them atop her head. "Just look at him," she said with a sigh. "Have you ever seen a more perfect man in your entire life?"

Gracie tore her gaze from the infant's serene face with apparent difficulty and squinted across the crowded beach. At the edge of the rushing water, Rick held Heather's hand and guided her toward an area where the surf was more gentle.

"Nope, can't say as I have." Gracie's pride in her son was evident. "If I'd found one, I'd have married him myself. Instead I had to take solace in creating him perfectly from scratch, then handing him over to someone else."

"And that someone else thanks you from the bottom of your heart. You did a magnificent job."

"Thank you, dear. You've done rather well yourself. Two incredibly beautiful children..." her voice broke slightly, "...makes a grandma proud."

A surge of warmth spread deep inside Catrina's chest. She automatically reached over to smooth the baby's blanket, caress her tiny cheek. "Sarina Leanne Blaine," she whispered. "I hope the world is as kind to you as it has been to your mom and big sister."

The baby blinked huge hazel eyes, blew a grinning bubble in response. Catrina kissed her sweet cheek, then turned her attention back to her precious firstborn, still happily cavorting with her doting adopted dad.

At five, Heather was sprouting taller each day, blossoming with a child-like hint of the beauty she would some day become. She was a daddy's girl like none that Catrina could ever imagine, watching the clock like a hungry hawk, then flinging herself into Rick's arms before he could so much as drop his briefcase, or shut the front door. Rick positively adored her.

He adored baby Sarina as well, even to the point of bashfully asking if the infant was old enough for formula so he could share in the feeding chores, just as he shared in all other facets of baby care. And that hadn't been his only suggestion.

"I might as well get used to floppy clothes," Catrina murmured aloud. "Rick was hinting last night about the girls needing a baby brother."

Grace chuckled. "If you expect me to discourage that line of thought, think again. The more the merrier."

"That's exactly what Rick said." Laughing, Catrina leaned back in her legless sand chair, adjusting the sun umbrella to shade out the glare. "My sister Laura is pregnant again, too."

"That's the one who lives in upstate New York with the millionaire who pretended not to like kids or cats, but ended up with an entire houseful of both?"

"Yep, that's the one. The best part is that Laura is expecting twins. Twins! Can you believe it? That will make four children, and they've barely been married four years."

Gracie slid Catrina a sly glance. "If you hurry, you can catch up with her."

"We've got plenty of time," Catrina murmured. "We've got forever."

"You say that as if you truly believe it."

"I believe it because it's true. Rick taught me that. He considers us to be soul mates, and you know what? We are. He's a part of me, the very best part of me, and deep inside I know that I'm the best part of him, too." Catrina scooped a handful of sand, let the grains run through her fingers.

For the first time in her life, she knew what it felt like to live the fantasies of her childhood. She and Laura were truly Cinderella sisters who had found the Prince Charmings of their dreams.

If only Susan could be so fortunate. But Susan had

never joined in the youthful dreams of her siblings, had never envisioned herself waiting for that princely steed to arrive bearing her own true love to carry her off in his arms.

She'd always been the pragmatist of the family. Catrina had once admired that; now she pitied it, because Susan had shielded herself against all marvelous possibilities. It takes courage to change, to risk everything and follow the whisper of one's heart. The rewards were beyond anything Catrina had ever imagined. True love wasn't a myth after all.

And forever was just the beginning.

* * * * *

Look for Susan Mitchell's story in the last book of Diana Whitney's STORK EXPRESS *series,*

THE NOT-SO-SECRET BABY,

in Silhouette Special Edition (#1373) coming January 2001.

Big Daddy Brubaker is back!
And this time his heart is set on getting
his three bachelor nephews hitched—any
way he can! Who will the lucky ladies be?
Find out in...

THE BRUBAKER BRIDES

by **Carolyn Zane**

THE MILLIONAIRE'S WAITRESS WIFE
(SR #1482, November 2000)

MONTANA'S FEISTY COWGIRL
(SR #1488, December 2000)

TEX'S EXASPERATING HEIRESS
(SR #1494, January 2001)

Watch for these uproariously funny
and wonderfully romantic tales...
only from Silhouette Romance!

Visit Silhouette at www.eHarlequin.com

SRBB

SILHOUETTE Romance

This Valentine's Day, fall in love with men you can tell your mother about!

Silhouette Romance introduces Cody, Alex and Jack, three men who make pulses pound and hearts race.

Make them a Valentine's Day gift to yourself!

BE MY BRIDE? by Karen Rose Smith
(SR#1492)
Sexy Cody Granger returns to his hometown, little girl in tow, proposing a marriage of convenience to Lauren MacMillan. Dare Lauren accept the loveless bargain?

SECRET INGREDIENT: LOVE by Teresa Southwick
(SR#1495)
Can intense businessman Alex Marchetti tempt chef Fran Carlino to whip up something especially enticing for two...?

JUST ONE KISS by Carla Cassidy
(SR#1496)
Little Nathaniel's impulsiveness gave Jack Coffey a broken leg. Would his lovely mother, Marissa Criswell, do even more damage to his heart?

Available at your favorite retail outlet.

Visit Silhouette at www.eHarlequin.com
SRVT

Silhouette®
Where love comes alive™

ATTENTION JOAN JOHNSTON FANS!

Silhouette Books is proud to present

HAWK'S WAY
BACHELORS

The first three novels in
the bestselling Hawk's Way series
now in one fabulous collection!

On Sale December 2000

THE RANCHER AND THE RUNAWAY BRIDE
Brawny rancher Adam Phillips has his hands full when
Tate Whitelaw's overprotective, bossy brothers show up with
shotguns in hand!

THE COWBOY AND THE PRINCESS
Ornery cowboy Faron Whitelaw is caught off-guard
when breathtakingly beautiful Belinda Prescott proves to be
more than a gold digger!

THE WRANGLER AND THE RICH GIRL
Sparks fly when Texas debutante Candy Baylor makes handsome
horse breeder Garth Whitelaw an offer he can't refuse!

**HAWK'S WAY: Where the Whitelaws of Texas
run free...till passion brands their hearts.**

"Joan Johnston does contemporary Westerns to perfection."
—Publishers Weekly

Available at your favorite retail outlet.

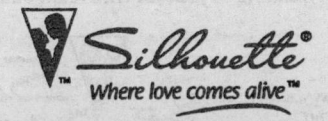

Silhouette®
Where love comes alive™

Visit Silhouette at www.eHarlequin.com

PSHWB

If you enjoyed what you just read, then we've got an offer you can't resist!

Take 2 bestselling love stories FREE!

Plus get a FREE surprise gift!

Clip this page and mail it to Silhouette Reader Service™

IN U.S.A.	IN CANADA
3010 Walden Ave.	P.O. Box 609
P.O. Box 1867	Fort Erie, Ontario
Buffalo, N.Y. 14240-1867	L2A 5X3

YES! Please send me 2 free Silhouette Romance® novels and my free surprise gift. Then send me 6 brand-new novels every month, which I will receive months before they're available in stores. In the U.S.A., bill me at the bargain price of $2.90 plus 25¢ delivery per book and applicable sales tax, if any*. In Canada, bill me at the bargain price of $3.25 plus 25¢ delivery per book and applicable taxes**. That's the complete price and a savings of at least 10% off the cover prices—what a great deal! I understand that accepting the 2 free books and gift places me under no obligation ever to buy any books. I can always return a shipment and cancel at any time. Even if I never buy another book from Silhouette, the 2 free books and gift are mine to keep forever. So why not take us up on our invitation. You'll be glad you did!

215 SEN C24Q
315 SEN C24R

Name _____ (PLEASE PRINT)

Address _____ Apt.#

City _____ State/Prov. _____ Zip/Postal Code

* Terms and prices subject to change without notice. Sales tax applicable in N.Y.
** Canadian residents will be charged applicable provincial taxes and GST.
All orders subject to approval. Offer limited to one per household.
® are registered trademarks of Harlequin Enterprises Limited.

SROM00_R ©1998 Harlequin Enterprises Limited

SILHOUETTE Romance™

Mature. Sophisticated. Experienced. Complex. A bit cynical. Every woman's dream man. Who else could it be but

AN OLDER MAN

Don't miss these stories from some of your favorite authors at Silhouette Romance!

In January 2001 Arlene James brings you
THE MESMERIZING MR. CARLYLE
Silhouette Romance #1493
Rich, enigmatic Reese Carlyle had no business pursuing Amber Presley. And then she learned his secret....

In February 2001 look for Valerie Parv's
BOOTIES AND THE BEAST
Silhouette Romance #1501
A tiny baby, an irresistible woman... has this gruff man met his match?

Available at your favorite retail outlet.

Silhouette®
Where love comes alive™

Visit Silhouette at www.eHarlequin.com.

SRAOM2

#1 *New York Times* bestselling author

NORA ROBERTS

brings you more of the loyal and loving, tempestuous and tantalizing Stanislaski family.

Coming in February 2001

The Stanislaski Sisters
Natasha and Rachel

Though raised in the Old World traditions of their family, fiery Natasha Stanislaski and cool, classy Rachel Stanislaski are ready for a *new* world of love....

And also available in February 2001 from Silhouette Special Edition, the newest book in the heartwarming Stanislaski saga

CONSIDERING KATE

Natasha and Spencer Kimball's daughter Kate turns her back on old dreams and returns to her hometown, where she finds the *man* of her dreams.

Available at your favorite retail outlet.

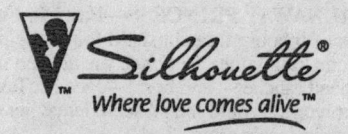

Silhouette
Where love comes alive™

Visit Silhouette at www.eHarlequin.com

PSSTANSIS

SILHOUETTE Romance

COMING NEXT MONTH

#1492 BE MY BRIDE?—Karen Rose Smith
Lauren MacMillan had never forgotten sexy Cody Granger. Then he returned to town, proposing a marriage of convenience to keep custody of his little girl. Dare Lauren trust Cody with the heart he had broken once before?

#1493 THE MESMERIZING MR. CARLYLE—Arlene James
An Older Man
He'd swept into her life, a handsome, charming, *wealthy* seafarer. But struggling single gal Amber Presley had no time for romance, though the mesmerizing Mr. Reece Carlyle seemed determined to make her his woman. Then she learned his secret motives....

#1494 TEX'S EXASPERATING HEIRESS—Carolyn Zane
The Brubaker Brides
She'd inherited a pig! And Charlotte Beauchamp hadn't a clue how to tame her beastly charge. Luckily, behaviorist Tex Brubaker sprang to her rescue. But his ultimate price wasn't something Charlotte was sure she could pay....

#1495 SECRET INGREDIENT: LOVE—Teresa Southwick
Businessman Alex Marchetti needed a chef, but was reluctant to hire beautiful and talented Fran Carlino. They'd both been hurt before in love, but their chemistry was undeniable. Could a confirmed bachelor and a marriage-shy lady find love and happiness together?

#1496 JUST ONE KISS—Carla Cassidy
Private investigator Jack Coffey claimed he was not looking for a family, but when he collided with little Nathaniel, he found one! As single mother Marissa Criswell nursed the dashing and surly man back onto his feet, she looked beyond his brooding exterior and tempted him to give her just one kiss....

#1497 THE RUNAWAY PRINCESS—Patricia Forsythe
Princess Alexis of Inbourg thought she'd found the perfect escape from her matchmaking father. But once she arrived in Sleepy River, she realized rancher—and boss!—Jace McTaggart was from a very different world. Would the princess leave her castle for a new realm—one in Jace's arms...?

CMN1200